The Strangers in Me
Jo Priestley

Copyright © 2023 Jo Priestley
All rights reserved.

Dedication

I never thought I'd write more than one book, yet here we are with book three of six (so far).

Thank you to the readers who provided invaluable feedback, some anonymously but the ones I know are Ann & Tracey. Thank you to Andrew for his superb editing skills and to Megan for adapting the book cover from an illustration by Alana Jordan.

My family are a constant support and a driving force to do my best. I always want to make them proud.

Chapter 1
1898—Annalise

Three pairs of eyes stare back at me as the train slows into the station.

I must tear my gaze away to see Donald the driver waving and beaming a smile at me under his veiny cheeks. I can only stand transfixed, bitter cold taking my breath, a scream sitting in a tight ball at the back of my throat.

Donald will be bewildered by my lack of response, but he must glance ahead to bring the train to a standstill. I see the smile slip from his face. Turning my head, we witness the same surreal scene together in the glow of the station lamplight.

But this is real, this is palpable.

I wanted to stay home tonight but Hugo insisted it was just nerves toying with me. I'm not his nursemaid he was quick to point out, and in any case, he had no need for one any longer; had I forgotten? Of course, I hadn't, it was just that sometimes I didn't want to leave, and my sick husband had been my excuse to stay.

Our home is elegant, but it's become a little tired of late. It's been slightly neglected and put on the backburner whilst more important matters were attended to. Wallpaper and soft furnishings have been the least of my worries. The slight neglect improves it to my mind, so it's cosier, more embracing. The piles of books and blankets waiting just in case they should be needed make it snug and less austere since the days when my mother and father-in-law used to live there. Then it was a museum, now I don't want to leave the manor as much as I don't want to leave my husband.

Hugo's thumb slid gently along my lower lip before he bent to kiss me. His palm nestling into the nape of my neck, and I closed my eyes. Maeve was clattering pots and pans in the scullery below, and Mrs Littlewood was scolding her for always behaving like a "clumsy clot of a girl."

The women's voices soon evaporated as I returned Hugo's kiss. He took me with him to that place of our own, that place meant only for us.

Studying his face when we pulled apart, I noticed the late autumn sun had restored the colour to his cheeks. The hollows above them have filled out to cradle his green eyes like before. The Hugo I know, and love has returned to me. Why would I want to leave; why would I want to travel hundreds of miles away from him?

"Perhaps a haircut might be in order before I return," I said, tousling his hair and smiling to soften my words.

When he scowled, I knew he wasn't cross.

"I thought you liked my longer curls," he said, "You told me they made me look rakish."

"Rakish was last week, my love, now you look like a mad axe murderer. You're on your way to terrifying small children."

Our carefree laughter joined. How I'd missed the simple sound of it. How I'd taken so much for granted.

"What do you plan to do to keep out of mischief until Tuesday?" I asked.

He rolled his eyes to the ceiling, pursing his lips.

"Let me see, well I suspect Veronica and Violet will keep me busy once they know the mistress of the house is absent once again," he said.

The unmarried twins from Kirkgate are always in their element spending time in my husband's company, both secretly holding a candle for him. I'm certain they're unaware it's not the best kept secret. The book study group was Violet's idea to talk all things literary with Hugo. She knew the way to his heart and so every Saturday morning until twenty-two months ago the twins and three other bookworms called in at the manor for tea and cake in our library. Now finally the study group can resume, and the twins will be clapping their hands with glee. They will fawn and hang onto Hugo's every word for two hours. He will be charming but, frustratingly for them, unbeguiled whilst he discusses the classics with the rest of the group. He will be articulate, knowledgeable and above all passionate about his much-loved subject. I can picture the scene.

I understand how the twins feel because he has an unsettling effect on women. I felt the same way once upon a time, but I was the lucky one. My feelings were reciprocated.

"I wish I could come with you like the old days," he said, his expression suddenly serious.

"Don't lie to me, Hugo, you hated me being the centre of attention, it drove you mad with jealously," I laughed.

Sighing theatrically, he said, "You're quite right of course, there's only room for one ego at Sutton Manor. We are different you and I, Annalise because you have talent and no ego whatsoever and I, well ..."

Nudging him playfully I knew he was using humour as a tried and tested disguise.

"I have every faith your work will be recognised one day. They will eventually see what I see, or should I say read what I read," I said.

I glanced over his shoulder at the grandfather clock in the hall, picking up my carpet bag and sliding on my gloves.

"I'll come with you," he said, reaching for his coat.

"No, the cold evening air will do nothing for your chest. You may be stronger but you're not better. I will be fine; you know I only need to walk to the gate at the rear of the manor and I managed perfectly well for five years if you remember."

"I love it when you play the school ma'am," he said, his eyes twinkling my way.

Shaking my head with a sigh, all I could do was give my husband one final kiss and close the door on our haven for three whole days.

Mrs Littlewood's voice floated up the cellar steps.

"Maeve, fetch the master's hot water stone from the cupboard. The weather's turned tonight so he'll be glad of it for bed," she said.

My stomach sank and my step faltered briefly. I wanted to be at home tending to Hugo, to fuss over him and check he had everything he needed before we retired for the night. This had been my role for so long. For two pins I could have turned on my heel and gone back inside.

Then I remembered people are waiting for me, and people haven't been waiting for me in a very long time.

Picking up speed at the thought I yomped down the gravel path to the gate, the brisk pace warming me up nicely.

"Oh, to be important enough to have your very own train stop. I hope the success doesn't go to your head, Annalise," mama said when I told her of the plans.

I doubt anyone would say success has gone to my head but after years of to-ing and froing between Yorkshire and London and the difficulty of getting to the mainline station in Leeds, it just seemed a practical and sensible proposal. The travelling was exhausting and I was not without means by then; so why not make life a little easier. And it meant I could spend a little more precious time with Hugo.

My agent Mr Bamford had suggested relocating to London but I just couldn't leave Yorkshire as much as he tried to persuade me. We had everything we needed and would have forever more, the money was there doing nothing so why not? How overindulgent it seems now, how positively vulgar even.

I covered my mouth to the rolling mist with my scarf. Sutcliffe had been out earlier to light the three lamps along the pathway and the only lamp of the station. Just a few short steps and I will be on my way back to my old life, I thought. Mr Bamford was due to meet me at Kings Cross to go in his carriage to my suite at the *Hotel Cecil* and discuss tomorrow's event. He will be as buoyant as the first time we met, his devotion to me unwavering.

I'd dilly dallied so long there were now only a couple of minutes to wait for the train. Sitting inside the small shelter I placed a welcome rug from my bag over my legs. Sutcliffe was insistent on accompanying me, but many things have changed at Sutton Manor.

"You have far too much to do I realise, Sutcliffe," I told him. If I can't walk a few steps beyond my own back garden, well, it's a poor show, don't you think?"

He stooped slightly, admitting defeat and a gentle smile appeared. His grey hair is gone at the crown, but the rest is always creamed and moulded to his head, so it doesn't look quite real. Sutcliffe was Hugo's father's butler before him and having been with Hugo his entire life they are inseparable to the extent that he usually knows what Hugo needs before he does.

"I'd rather the circumstances were different, madam, but it has indeed been a pleasure having you home more."

The circumstances he referred to, well, they've been a trial, a trauma even, but they've also been the making of me and cemented my love for my husband. I realise now how love is taken for granted in good times.

Staring through the window of the shelter I had a clear view of the line and I thought of the last time I sat here waiting, without a care in the world.

"Annalise," a voice sprang from the silence, and I knew immediately it was mama though I couldn't see her.

"Mama, what are you doing out here at this time of night …"

My words travelled into the darkness. Out of the shadows she appeared Sissy and Lilian. The look on their faces made me scramble to my feet, discarding the rug carelessly on the damp floorboards of the shelter.

I heard a voice, familiar yet strange, different to what I'd come to know.

"I'm telling you right now, we're not leaving here until you've told her the truth. You just can't help spewing lies, endless lies and it's got to stop tonight. They've become second nature to you and I can't take it any longer, do you hear me?"

I knew who it was but the sound was warped with venom. I hadn't a clue what was going on, but a growing sense of fear crawled across my body. I took a step toward the group to get a better look and saw my mother shake her head, her eyes pleading with me to go no further. In the gaslight, her gaze led me to an orangey glint of a blade .

In that moment I heard the first sounds of the locomotive, wheezing its way up the line to our stop; Donald, our engine driver, oblivious to what lies ahead.

We are now frozen in time like a sinister still life; certain in the knowledge that any sudden movement could have horrific consequences.

Oh, Donald my friend, you have no idea right now how much I need you to be my knight in shining armour charging to our rescue. Only you can save us.

Chapter 2

1869—The Whitworths

How to handle this delicately, Garrison Whitworth wonders as he snuffs out the candle of his office to draw a line under another day. His nightly routine is as reliable as the town hall clock: he indulges in one last look around the room, revelling in the sense of order. He has a set position for everything on his desk and on his shelves and it pleases him immensely. It gives him a sense of peace, of calm.

But not tonight.

Smoothing down his moustache as he makes his way to the stairs, the pleasing smell of sawn wood greets him. It's his favourite smell and stems from visiting the mill as a child when his father was the one in charge. This night though he pays little heed as his mind replays the conversation that he had only moments ago.

Stevie's revelation has taken his breath away and an opportunity seems to have just landed in his lap from nowhere when he wasn't looking. Stevie was certain the girl would be open to the idea, and Stevie wouldn't give him false hope, not Stevie, he was too level-headed. He'd been with him since he was a scraggy-arsed fourteen-year-old, scurrying in the other direction when Garrison strode down the corridor. Of course, there'd been plenty of apprentices before and since but none who had affected him quite the same. He was different; he didn't know why exactly but the heart speaks a language all of its own.

He'd heard his heart speak to him with Clara. She's a plain Jane to others, he knows it but never to him. He sees beneath the veneer of people. Garrison was surprised more than anyone about how she made such an impact because back then he was a man's man, women a mere diversion. Yet when his father introduced her as his second cousin come visiting from Richmond, he had a stirring which never quite settled again. And Clara never went home again.

They married within six months, a quiet wedding at Clara's insistence because she doesn't like a lot of fuss, and they lived at Hardcastle House, with his parents, until they died. His father died of a heart episode and his mother of gastric complications. It was likely the result of high-living. They loved the high life—good food, fine wine, the best cigars for his father. Money came to them later in life as his carpentry business took off, borne on the winds of commerce and growth in the local towns. It was clear they felt they should make up for lost time. Garrison thinks about his parents often; he misses them.

Before he died, his father asked him when he was to become a grandpa.

"I'm not getting any younger, son," he said with a twinkle in his eye.

"Give us chance papa, the ink on the church register is barely dry," Garrison said, laughing.

His father raised his brandy glass and Garrison did the same as they shared a knowing smile.

Three months turned to nine and the joke lessened little by little until it soured completely and ran away to hide in the dark corners of their minds. He and Clara talked about it at first then they began to be uncomfortable bringing it up.

They had made many trips to Harley Street, the doctors telling them tales of couples who had tried for years for a baby then succeeded. They meant well wanting to give them some hope, some comfort but it didn't succeed. Years was not an appealing concept when waiting days was all-consuming enough.

Something has kept him believing he will be a father one day, however. He's always known one day it would happen because he dreamt it. He never saw the face of the child, but it was undoubtably his as the sensation of them belonging to him was profound. He woke with tears in his eyes and reached for Clara to allay her fears. Then he thought better of it as he realised that he couldn't explain how real it had felt and, in any case why would she place her faith in a dream.

From that night he knew it was only a matter of time before he became a father because Garrison Whitworth thinks of dreams differently to others.

To him, dreams are simply premonitions.

*

Perhaps I misheard, Clara thinks, twirling her wedding band manically around her finger. Why would anyone do such a thing?

"Are you listening to me, Clara?" Garrison asks, leaning across to take her hand.

She nods, her round, glazed eyes staring through him.

"I am dear, of course but I can't take it in," she says.

He remains silent waiting for her to come back to him. She returns slowly to stare at their two hands clasped in a love knot on her lap. Anxiety is always sitting in Clara but sometimes it can swipe her from the side like tonight so she must sit down.

Her husband's hope is her hope and it's burning brightly telling her their prayers have been answered. Yet, she knows this hope is far too premature. There are untold obstacles to overcome for him to drop such a heavy load of expectation in her lap.

"Stevie told me the girl's terrified, absolutely desperate. Don't you see if we brought her to the house under the guise of a live-in, her parents would not suspect a thing. She could then be 'let go' in due course."

How simple and straightforward the plan seems, Clara thinks. She stands to pace the floor because she must distance herself from the need in his eyes which is stifling her. She resumes twirling her ring making her finger red and sore but still she can't stop.

"I think you have me at a disadvantage, my love, I need time to digest your words because this is not a step to be taken lightly."

He rolls his hands down his handsome face, turning a shade pinker.

"Clara, Clara, Clara, time is not on our side. If we don't act quickly the opportunity will slip from our grasp. I'm not sure I can bear it … but more to the point, I'm not sure you can bear it."

She folds her new bottle-green woollen skirt under her before sitting down. Clara has many clothes but as her father said, you can't make a silk purse out of a sow's ear. To her mind, she could have all the embellishment in the world but sadly would still remain invisible to most, but somehow not to Garrison. Garrison makes her feel alluring, seductive even, words she had read in her novels but never experienced. The feeling is intoxicating, like a drug. She can't lose it and if she falters, she might. If they should lose this once in a lifetime opportunity she could, perish the thought, lose her husband. Her soulmate.

Garrison's eyes are glued to his wife's face, trying to gauge her thoughts as they unravel. He's trying to give her time, but impatience is only making him grind his teeth.

Finally, Clara drops her head back and heaves a great sigh.

"If you think that you and Stevie can make this happen then of course you must," she says.

Garrison springs from his seat then flopping to his knees he hugs her tightly just like when he proposed. Oh, the joy of a man like him proposing to a girl like her, professing his undying love not only for a while but forever.

Clara's heart flutters with a sudden realisation: to a child their mother is their world, she would be placed at the heart of their entire world.

Never again would she feel invisible.

Chapter 3

1869—Lilian

Lilian drops the curtain when she sees Stevie coming through the gate to the back yard.

He's clutching an armful of wood cuttings from the workshop at Whitworth's and he's trying to protect it from the driving rain. Her mother tells him every time he comes, she doesn't know how she'd manage without the fuel in winter, and every time Stevie blushes.

Since their father died, Mr Whitworth insisted they have the off cuts. He didn't know her father, nor her mother, but he knew she was a widow who lived on the opposite side of the street with two young girls to support. He became their benefactor and how kind he was to think of them they all agreed.

"It would only go to waste, Mrs Reid," Stevie said the first time he called.

Lilian and Sissy have been friends with Stevie since school. He'd secured a prestigious apprenticeship to an experienced joiner at Garrison Whitworth & Sons Ltd whilst they'd gone to work at Earnshaw's as trainee seamstresses. A seamstress sounded a grand title, and it certainly was a job where you could move up the ranks with ease if you arrived on time and kept your powder dry.

Sissy is only thirteen months older than Lilian, but because she's the oldest, Sissy managed to rise up the ranks quicker. It was only right she went from buttonholing to proper sewing before her younger sister. Lilian accepted her fate without question, even though she was a better seamstress, because she understood there's a natural order of things.

Every Friday they tip up most of their earnings to their mother, keeping back a little pocket money, and she clinks it into the little red tin on the mantlepiece.

"By that's a satisfying sound," Sissy said the first Friday they did it and her sister nodded in agreement. They were proud to finally be in a position to help their mother who'd been struggling to make ends meet. She never grumbled so neither did they, even when they had to look on as the posh children devoured paper bags of fancy sweets on a Saturday afternoon. Stevie would occasionally give them a piece of toffee, but they wouldn't let him buy them their own or this would be charity. His bag used to get a bit bigger every week, Lilian remembers.

Their house is the end terrace on Bright Eye Lane. Lilian often wonders if it was the original name of the street, or one the Whitworth's made up to be a talking point. Nobody knew the answer when she asked but everyone loved to say they lived on Bright Eye Lane. Old Mr Whitworth had a new cobbled street laid and arranged for the houses to be painted every September before the winter set in. After he died, young Mr Whitworth continued this tradition, which made him instantly popular with the tenants. Inside, the houses are neat as a pin because folk here have a certain pride about keeping up appearances. People on the lane are sniffy if anyone doesn't peg their curtains and nets out to dry at least once every season ... and people keep count.

Lilian couldn't care less about curtains and nets. She used to like to play on the street with the boys until she started work and always came home clarted with mud if it was raining, or snagged tights. Why she couldn't wear trousers like the boys was beyond her.

"Lilian, you are a girl, and you must accept the differences between boys and girls. One day you'll be glad of them, mark my words," her mother told her.

She had a funny smile on her face when she said it Lilian thought. But then her mother was often smiling.

"Mrs Reid, Sissy, Lilian," Stevie says, nodding his head at each of them in turn, cap in hand.

"Sit down, lad," Elspeth says, "I'll get your tea—chocolate cake today, Stevie."

How Stevie loves the cosy little kitchen. He's been coming for nearly four years twice a week and every time he never wants to leave. Since his mother died, he lives with his father and two brothers, so a feminine touch is never part of his house like it is at No 2. Little things like the fire always blazing, more than just one candle being lit at dusk, doyleys under cups, but it's the smell he likes best of all; the smell of home as he thinks of it. The aroma is smoke from the fire mixed with soap and baking. He'd once tried to replicate it at home by baking a sponge cake and his father and brothers had taken the rise out him so much, he was never fool enough to do it again. Baking is women's work they scoffed. They live off stews, pies, and bread, and with four wages coming in they buy them from the baker. Sadly, money doesn't buy you a home only a house Stevie knows now.

    Lilian looks at Stevie side on whilst he chats to her mother. He's a good-looking lad with gingery hair and blue eyes surrounded by blonde eyelashes and crowned with eyebrows of the same colour. His eyes stray her way and she looks at the fire quickly, her cheeks flooding with colour. Sissy was smitten with him, but she married Samuel a year ago which was a shock to them at the time because Sam was known for his fiery temper. Sissy said it didn't worry her as she knew how to handle him and anyway, she could never marry a boring man. Is Stevie boring, Lilian wonders? She has no idea but she knows he's Mr Whitworth's favourite according to the other lads so he must have something. They call him *Golden Boy* which is quite fitting really with his colouring.

    Stevie continued coming week after week, month after month with the wood and Elspeth continued to fuss and cluck over him.

    Although Lilian was often around and looked forward to his visits, she didn't get to find out if he was boring to live with or otherwise. She did however find out the differences between boys and girls eventually.

    But unlike her mother, she didn't think it was anything to smile about.

Chapter 4

1869—The Whitworths

Clara leans against the wall soaking up the atmosphere of the room in the silence.

How she wishes she could have spoken to her mother about getting ready for the new baby. This was impossible so she used her gumption to work it out. Garrison said they should really wait to find a nanny just in case. This was understandable, she thought. It hadn't been easy, but the result is breath-taking, a sweet little room fit for a prince … or princess.

Staring at the new rocking chair by the cradle she pictures herself with a baby nestling in her arms. This is dangerous she knows but she can't help it.

The girl who is having the baby has a name now, she's known it for some time: Lilian. A pretty little brown-haired thing from nowhere. Garrison didn't tell her where she was from, and Clara didn't ask. These things are better left to the imagination because she doesn't want to think of Lilian in a house, sitting by the fire with her mother and father who will be the child's grandparents. She doesn't want to know where she lives in case she's tempted to loiter outside her house one day. If she does that, she might find out too much about her life. No, the less she knows about the girl the better and in her mind, she will always be just that: *The Girl.*

"You know, we haven't thought things through properly, Clara," Garrison said to her one morning in bed.

He'd just made love to her the way she loved, building steadily to take them to the height of their passion. Garrison never rushes their lovemaking, always very present and attentive. He buried his face in her neck to breathe her scent, the scent he bought her every Christmas and birthday, so she never ran out. His trail of kisses ran from her neck to her breasts, a light flick of his tongue on her nipple making her gasp. He likes her to gasp, it makes him feel powerful. Further and further his lips lowered until his breath was between her legs and she moaned knowing the pleasure instore for her. When he raised his head to stare at her she felt hot under his gaze. She's unable to comprehend how fresh their lovemaking feels, never falling short in intensity, the sensation only growing over time. As their love layers, so does their desire it seems. She looks forward to being alone with him, being his and he hers for a while.

Laying with her head on his chest he stroked her shoulder.

What hadn't they thought about? She was suddenly worried he was having second thoughts. If he backtracks now, she will have to challenge him for once as she's too far down the road.

"I mean discretion is paramount. The girl cannot come here pregnant even if we hid her in the attic, heaven forbid. I think she should live elsewhere until the baby arrives and then the servants will never question anything when we tell them we've adopted a baby. It will just be her word against ours if the plan goes awry," he said craning his neck to look at her.

Clara wriggled free to sit up and pulled the sheet under her arms to protect her modesty. Though she was relieved he was still supportive, the magnitude of the situation was making her feel quite sick. She assumed there would be some sort of agreement drawn up at least so the girl could never make a claim for her baby in the future. If not she's at risk of the child being ripped from her arms at any moment. To live with the constant fear of that happening would be unbearable.

"For some reason I thought you would be trying to formalise the arrangement," she said clamping her palm to her forehead, "Surely, this would be the best option for everyone involved."

Rolling himself out of bed Garrison slipped on his robe, brushing his hair back with his hands. How appealing he always looks on a morning even when dishevelled Clara thought. She tidied her hair quickly with her fingers, glad of the semi-gloom of the bedroom.

"You're quite right, I'll draft something tomorrow, nothing fancy to risk scaring her off, however. I'll show you the draft to get your thoughts before I give it to her."

Clara could finally breathe again.

She knew such a document would never stand up in court, but the girl wouldn't know that.

"Stevie told me the girl enjoyed taking long walks with her father before he died, up to Haigh and back. It's near her sister apparently so that's probably a good thing. Old Dick Tanner has a nice little cottage he'd be willing to rent out, no questions asked. He didn't say that of course, he only said he didn't care if I kept pigs in it so long as I paid the rent. Funny old chap.

Clara didn't know the village or anyone living there which was good, she thought.

So, it seems it's all planned out and the dream is to become a reality for them both. A reality where they have a cradle and teddy bears and little wooden building blocks with letters of the alphabet artfully painted on them.

Laying on the nursery rug she lets the tufts of soft wool slip through her fingers as she studies the intricate beams of the ceiling. Hardcastle is a truly beautiful house, and it's become her life's work. She never forgets what a refuge it was when she needed it so suddenly.

Clara's mother had lived in a tiny cottage on the estate until her death. It's almost derelict now and she doesn't like to pass it on her walks because she pictures her mother sitting by the range, telling and retelling memories of her childhood as though she was going slowly mad. Guilt had consumed her at the end and the worst of it was, her mother knew her father would not be waiting for her on the other side.

When Clara came here Garrison turned out to be just the distraction she needed. He understood her homesickness for Richmond because even now he could never leave Hardcastle. The same went for his parents who were alive at the time; they were very tightly knit as a family and Clara envied that. If they were to be together, she would have to up sticks and move across the country to create a brand-new life. It couldn't have happened at a better time.

Does she have what it takes to be a good mother? This question is plaguing Clara of late, often keeping her awake at night. She already thinks of the baby as her own so she's hoping a certain instinct will kick in just when she needs it like with any new mother. She knows she is sorely lacking in experience with babies in general so she plans to employ the best nanny they can find and then just pick it up as she goes along.

Rising to her feet she decides to sit in the rocking chair by the tiny attic window. She has a perfect view of the crags at the back of the house glistening with snow, clouds foaming from the tops like frothy suds.

At first, she wanted the nursery to be next to their bedroom but then she thought the nearness of a baby might change things with her husband. Intimacy is of the utmost importance not only to Garrison but to Clara too. She wants to please her husband daily; this unspoken rule has been woven into the fabric of their marriage and she was a willing weaver.

So much change is afoot, this is surely the calm to relish before the storm, but she believes passionately that Hardcastle is ready for a child to sprinkle a little magic onto daily life.

She hears the distant chime of the clock in the hall calling her downstairs for tea. Reluctant to leave she plumps the cushion in the rocking chair, restoring the room to perfection and closes the door on the nursery until tomorrow. Making her way down the chilly landing, she touches the face just for luck of the portrait of Old Whitty. This is their affectionate name for him, and the habit has become her little ritual. His formal pose belies his gentle kindness she always thinks. His face is taut, his posture stiff and rigid and in his best Sunday attire he looks austere when he was really very approachable. Garrison sits in his own portrait to his father's right, but a different artist was better able to capture her husband's spirit, she thinks. He isn't smiling but he has a look in his eye which she often sees in real life.

No doubt one day their child will join them in the gallery: three generations of Whitworth's watching over these four walls forever. Clara crosses her fingers and sighs, hoping her wish will come true.

Who knew when mother bundled her into the carriage all those years ago, she would become lady of the manor? The family were in dire straits and Old Whitty, her mother's cousin had been only too happy to come to their rescue. He hadn't expected Clara to arrive and swoop his son off his feet.

Only two weeks before they came, Clara's father had left the family disgraced and on the brink of the workhouse. That awful day when they left the courthouse, Clara and her mother were heckled and spat at by a baying mob. They shouldn't have gone but naively, thought he would get a reprieve at the eleventh hour. Her father's barrister had misled them with talk of it being a 'crime of passion' but in the end he wasn't spared the noose.

The victim was her mother's lover, a fact her mother carefully omitted from the tale she told Old Whitty because he may not have been so accommodating had he known. Instead, she told him her husband had landed himself in debtor's prison after some investment opportunities had gone sour. Clara was choked with guilt when he almost fell over himself to help the two terrified, destitute women.

But what other option did her mother have?

To this very day Garrison junior has no idea whatsoever that his mousy little wife has such a macabre history.

Chapter 5

1869—Lilian

A scented handkerchief can't prevent Lilian retching at the stench. The smell is unmistakable—animal faeces—and it looks to be crusted to the stone flags of the kitchen floor.

"Well, it is an old farm cottage, Lily but it only needs some soap and water," Stevie says optimistically, rolling up the sleeves of his overalls, "With a bit of elbow grease we'll have it like a little palace in no time."

Stuffing her handkerchief in her bag Lilian manages a weak smile though her bottom lip trembles. I should be at home with mam now she thinks, not here cleaning up a midden. It's Monday so they'd be having liver with onions and mash for tea and then afterward they would crochet some festive gifts by the cosy glow of the kitchen fire. The nights are drawing in and the run up to Christmas is Lilian's favourite time of year.

Has she lost her mind to be going along with this plan? She would snatch an alternative solution and run like the wind if she could only think of it. This deception has become a terrible burden; she never even told a white lie to her mother before now.

Lilian Reid, she scolds herself in her mind, before was another world away from all this, you must bite the bullet and get on with it.

She has so much to thank Stevie for; and this enormous debt of gratitude only adds to the weight on her shoulders. He had told Mr Whitworth he would clean and whitewash the cottage before Lilian moved in to avoid having to involve anyone else.

Thank goodness for this man, she thinks as she watches him pick up a brush to sweep the flags. He's been her guardian angel since that sunny afternoon in the height of a summer heatwave. Lilian pictures herself running after him down the street, skirts high, perspiring from heat and nerves. She wanted to try and catch him before she lost her nerve and he disappeared into the depths of Whitworth's workshop. The other children were paying them no heed, absorbed in their carefree fun and games as she called out his name.

When he spun on his heel, he immediately took off his cap. The act was as instinctive as breathing because he considers himself nothing if not courteous and civil. Her mother has a word for Stevie: endearing she called him, and Lilian thought it a very apt description at that moment.

"Lily, what's the matter?" he asked taking in the urgency on her face.

She was Lily to him in his mind but always Lilian in front of her mother.

Gesturing with her head for him to follow her to the side of the privy row Lilian tapped each of the five doors in turn. They must be alone for this conversation. The spot was far from ideal but at least they were out of sight of Whitworth's and more importantly, out of sight of her house.

Stevie's front tooth was embedded in his bottom lip. Trouble was afoot, he knew it. He knew Lilian, she wasn't one for drama.

"I'm sorry for all the mystery, Stevie but I… I'm in trouble and I need your help. You're the only person I can trust not to say anything."

She didn't say he was the only person who could help but somehow, she just knew he would.

The sigh escaping him was so loud it startled Lilian almost as much as it did himself. He realised he'd been holding his breath for too long. Sliding his cap back on he gave her his full attention trying to decipher the meaning behind her unexpected appearance. His mind turned, trying to pre-empt the reason she needed him to lend an ear when she never had before.

It only took a moment for him to wish he hadn't tried.

Lilian watched his Adam's apple bob up and down as she couldn't meet his eyes.

"You're not … you're not in the worst kind of trouble Lily, are you?" he asked, leaning against the wall. He suddenly needed to steady himself, realising he was out of his depth.

Lilian dropped her head to her chest but didn't respond. The silence twisted itself around them like barbed wire.

Oh, Lily he thought, you're too good for this. For goodness sake, you had the world at your feet with your mother behind you, how could you be so bloody stupid? You may as well have thrown your mother's good heart on the ground and trampled it.

"Do I know the father?" he asked.

His words came out a touch more bluntly than he would have liked. Lilian couldn't help but be wounded by the tone of his voice as he'd never been anything other than pleasant with her. She still couldn't look at him as the sounds of the street became muted by the blood swimming in her ears.

"It's somebody from work; it's not straightforward," she said quietly.

Stevie's mind ran ahead, so he had to catch up with it.

"He's not ...married, is he?"

She shook her head but didn't give him the answer he wanted.

"Look I'd like to tell you who it is, but I can't, Stevie. The less you know the better. Anyway, it's me who needs your help not him."

She does need my help he thought whether I like it or not. He sighed, the fire now going from his belly and reached to put his hand lightly on her arm.

He was thrown when she grabbed his fingers suddenly and clung tightly to them and a heat ran up his chest. At that moment he realised the person in front of him wasn't a villain, someone to demonise, just a young, foolish girl, frightened of what lay ahead for her. Not the first, and not the last, he thought.

His arms curled around her of their own accord, and she buried her head in his chest to block out the world—her world, on her street.

"Look, let me have a think," he said, "I'm not sure yet how I can help but I might be able to come up with something."

"Are you absolutely sure," Stevie asked, knowing it was a pointless question.

"As I can be," Lily replied flatly.

Deep in thought his chin rested on top of her head. Her brown hair smelt clean, her small frame stirring an undeniable protective instinct. She needed him and this was new and unsettling, but how he'd hate to let Lilian down. How he'd hate to let the family down.

Like everyone else, Stevie had heard tales of desperation about young girls in her shoes. He must think of a way forward because this was not an option for her.

Could he marry her? He'd never given any thought to the question though he liked her well enough. Of course, he could, but he had barely enough money for a wife and child. He could help her, but he wasn't in a position to marry her.

The two Barker brothers appeared around the corner to use the toilet and Lilian pulled away, embarrassed to be caught in such a way. She knew it was silly as the boys were too young to care or even notice that the couple had their arms around each other.

As Stevie turned to walk behind Lilian and back into the sunshine of Bright Eye Lane, he felt a sadness weighing down his heart.

Yet he knew that however hard it was for him it was nothing compared to the turmoil that must be going on in Lilian's mind.

Lily, head bowed, felt the shame of the encounter had changed her in few short minutes.

And changed her for good.

*

Whitworth's is completely deserted except for the great man himself. Garrison Whitworth on the top floor checking over the contract for a shopfitting job in Manchester. It's a new department store, and the cabinetry alone will take six months at least to complete. He's used to winning contracts but even so he can't abide complacency and he's never greedy. He has the same enthusiasm for every project, and this is why the company is invariably chosen over others, and even starting to be noticed outside the county.

It took his father twenty-five years to grow the business from his start as a jobbing carpenter, touring the towns and villages for work. Garrison remembers him heading off when he was a small child, toolbox in hand. Such was his workmanship that he was able to put down roots in the town and employ four carpenters, whilst still remaining hands on himself. Then four carpenters became eight and the family moved from their cottage on the outskirts of Leeds to one of the new town houses in the suburbs.

It was the 'big job' that did it, the job which changed everything. It was the shopfitting contract his father won for the first department store in Leeds. This magnificent palace of commerce had everything under one roof and crowds came just to see it for months after the grand opening. The oak panelling and mahogany display cases also brought his father's work to the attention of a new and growing commercial clientele. After that, his father never looked back. He bought the premises Garrison sits in now and finally exchanged his overalls for a suit. Two years later they moved into Hardcastle and began living the highlife with gusto, making up for lost time.

The day his father died Garrison wept as much about the weight of responsibility now squarely on his shoulders as he did for the loss of his best friend. One minute he was there for him to lean on, the next he was being carried out of the house with a sheet covering his face.

Was he up to the job was the question that hounded him as he climbed into bed beside Clara that night.

By the time he got up the following morning he was a different man. From that day he picked up the baton and ran with it using all his charisma and powers of persuasion to win the best contracts. But when he won them, he followed through because his father employed the most skilled men he could find, and Garrison did the same. He pays good money and by example treats the men well. But he expects a good day's work and the highest standards. Now he has his pick of men working on and off site as they clamour to work for the mighty Whitworths.

Garrison checks his fob watch and decides in five more minutes to head home a little earlier to surprise Clara.

Downstairs Stevie is pacing the floor, weaving amongst the work benches. He snuck in the back door after he counted the staff leaving one by one, watching on from the disused outhouse. He had to be certain he and Garrison would be alone. Mrs Wagstaff the cleaner isn't due for another hour, so the coast is clear. Now is the time.

But time to do what? Knock on the door and tell Mr Whitworth the daughter of the family across the way is up the spout. What is it to Garrison Whitworth; what is he supposed to do about it?

He and Garrison have always had a very amiable working relationship, especially since his apprenticeship ended, but this is a huge leap, a liberty even. He wouldn't want to spoil the affinity he has with his employer.

Then he thinks of Lily nestling in his arms, her tiny head on his chest like a little injured bird with nobody to save it. You can save her, Stevie if you take this first step. If you're careful how you approach it, then there will be no harm done even if he won't or can't help. He trusts Garrison he realises, which is odd when he has no basis for it, no proof. It's more an instinct.

Twice Stevie stands with his hand poised mid-air by the huge oak door of Garrison's office. Both times he drops it and walks away only to go back again. The third time he's annoyed with himself and without hesitation knocks on the door. He smooths his red hair with his palms and straightens the collar of his overalls as he waits.

"Come in!" shouts the voice from beyond the doors.

Garrison sits back in his seat and smiles spontaneously when he sees who it is. He thought it was Mrs Wagstaff come early due to some domestic commitment or other she often had so this is a surprise.

"What brings you here at this time of night, Stevie?" he asks, "You should be away home for your supper like everybody else."

Stevie doesn't answer, he only stands tongue-tied with a strange expression Garrison has never seen before. When Stevie remains rooted to the spot, Garrison notices his pale complexion is almost lucid tonight. Something is wrong.

Is his father ill, perhaps his brothers, Garrison wonders now. Leaving his desk, he strides over to the wingback chairs by the fire. They're barely used but the desk is no place to have this kind of conversation, he knows it already.

"Come on now, sit down, lad," he says, "You look like you need to afore you fall down."

Stevie is fighting the urge to make an excuse and leave, but after a few seconds he somehow manages to take the first step of the long walk to sit opposite his big gaffer as he thinks of him. He can't seem to stop his body quivering and the fire is no use as he's not cold. He hasn't felt so out of control since his mother died of influenza and his older brother Dennis told him he had to "man up" because his father had enough on his plate without needing to listen to him snivelling.

Garrison goes to the drinks cabinet by the window and pours two large brandies into fine crystal glasses. He hands one to Stevie, who can only stare at it.

"Take it, the first sip is the worst and each one after that gets better you mark my words.

Stevie has two tiny sips then realising he doesn't mind the taste takes a strong gulp. The warmth travels swiftly down his gullet and after a small cough he can't deny the sensation somehow makes him feel better, calmer.

Watching on from his chair Garrison sits crossed-legged, brandy in one hand, thumb and forefinger rubbing his bearded chin with the other.

"So, what brings you here to see me tonight?" he asks finally.

Stevie's turquoise eyes are huge, his blonde lashes in the firelight creating a halo effect around them. Garrison's ankle twitches manically as he waits.

"Stevie lad you have nothing to fear from me. If you're in a spot of bother, you can tell me."

Stevie finishes his brandy and sets the glass down on the side table. Come on now, Stephen, he cajoles himself, get a grip of yourself.

"Mr Whitworth, you don't know how hard it is for me to come to you with this … problem, but I must try everything I can for peace of mind. It's not me who's in a spot of bother, in trouble … it's the young lass opposite. Lilian, the one who lost her father eight years or more back."

Garrison's lower lip drops slightly; he doesn't understand why Stevie should be getting so worked up about the girl opposite. He sits awhile with his thoughts before he speaks. Though he wonders why Stevie should turn to him for help, he can't deny he's secretly pleased he felt he could.

Suddenly his racing mind sets off on a tangent in another direction.

"I see," Garrison says, "and I take it you are the father."

Stevie looks horrified, like he's thrown his brandy in his face.

"No, oh god, no. I never thought about you thinking that. I'm just worried about her, and I'm worried about her mother finding out too. She's got enough to contend with being a widow and a mother when money's tight."

Garrison smiles affectionately across at Stevie. He's a thinker this one, a worrier, the boys obviously grown fond of the family since he's been taking them the wood.

"Stevie, you've got a heart of gold you have lad. I saw it when I first met you," Garrison says, almost breaking into a laugh. " Remember how you tried to protect old Tordoff, because you thought I was going to lay him off."

Stevie stares at the fire, his heart buckling at the memory of his late foreman. If he'd still been alive, he might have chosen to speak to him about Lilian rather than Garrison, but Mr Tordoff went from bad to worse with his aches and pains. Then one morning Garrison came into the workshop and announced he died in the night and there would be a collection for his widow.

Dead—Mr Tordoff was dead. The word rang round Stevie's head for months. If he'd talked to Garrison about how the old man was struggling instead of covering it up, he might still be alive, but Mr Tordoff had made him promise. It was a hard lesson learned young.

Garrison stares at Stevie's profile, his hair aglow from the firelight. This was the last thing he expected to be discussing this evening. Stevie's clearly upset, and the thought of two teenagers, one motherless, one fatherless alone in such a predicament is upsetting him too.

The man and boy sit in an uneasy silence by the fireside, but Stevie feels lighter for offloading the problem. This room feels like a safe place, he'd like to stay here so he doesn't need to face the harsh realities with the young girl over the road. He imagines Lilian barely sleeping tonight, waiting for news. It looks like there might be nothing to report after all, so he'll have to come up with another solution.

Garrison feels a sudden shift at a realisation. He shuffles forward in his seat, his body almost itching with a sense of anticipation. Of course, it's all so obvious.

Stevie is suddenly aware that the mood has changed and looks his way wondering what's afoot, on edge for what will be coming any second now. Garrison is carefully formulating a plan; he has never been more certain of anything in his life. Except Clara.

Stevie is completely oblivious, but some higher power sent this golden-haired boy to him tonight Garrison thinks. He feels it to his very core like a mother's kiss.

This boy was sent this night to make all his dreams, all his premonitions come true.

Chapter 6

1869—Sissy

Sissy cocks her well-tuned ear when she hears the gate go. Sometimes she thinks Samuel deliberately opens it quietly to try and catch her in the act of goodness knows what. She's no idea how that man's mind works.

She pounces into action, herding Jack and Harry like sheep with her arms and shooing them in the direction of the stairs.

"Up you go, boys," she says, and her two sons do her bidding without question as always. It's almost like an army drill, ingrained into their routine so they don't even think about it.

Throwing their small collection of toys hurriedly into the old apple crate she keeps under the stairs she glances around to check everything else is as it should be. Sissy is worn out after her daily chores most nights, but pure adrenaline is the perfect injection of energy she needs.

Samuel will call later for his usual three pints at *The Crooked Billet* after tea. Three is just enough to knock the edge off but not so much he loses control or too much of his hard-earned wages. He comes home earlier than most men because of it and her friends and neighbours consider her a lucky girl to have such a considerate husband.

She hears him kicking off his boots in the passageway and the drop of his clothes on the tiles. He appears around the door in his underwear waiting until Sissy tops up his bath by the fireside with hot water from the kettle.

"Hello, love," Sissy greets him.

She never asks if he's had a good day because he hasn't. Who would have a good day sweating like a pig with coal dust clinging to their throat and lungs? He'd pointed this out about two weeks after they'd wed when he couldn't stand hearing the question any longer. She felt small and silly for asking. It was the simple question her mother asked her father when he came home from work so Sissy followed suit. But her father didn't hate his job because he was a leather worker, light pouring into the giant tannery windows all day long.

How Sissy missed her father at that moment and couldn't help comparing Samuel to him. He fell short: she never heard her father speak to her mother in such a way.

Her mother called with Lilian earlier and they had Eccles cakes Elspeth made especially because she knows they're Sissy's favourite. She's thoughtful, always thinking about her girls with little gestures that don't go unnoticed.

"Stan says your mam and Lil came earlier," Samuel says, sliding into the warm water.

Handing him the soap Sissy tells him, "Yes, mam brought you some macaroons, you can have them after tea."

43

Building a lather between his filthy hands he washes the coal dust from his hair and face as Sissy scrubs his back. She is waiting. Samuel never says anything on a whim, no passing comment or remark would ever fall from his lips. Her mouth is dry, her stomach curdling with nerves.

The black water splashes over the tin bath as he stands to wrap a warmed towel around his waist. Sissy has laid his clothes out neatly in a pile by the hearth.

"Must be nice to sit around gabbing and supping tea while your man's scrabbling around in the earth to earn a crust for the family," he says.

She doesn't answer. Sometimes this tack works and other times it doesn't. The unpredictability is the worst, not knowing how to respond from one day to the next. If it wasn't this that irritated him, it would be something else.

Closing her eyes, Sissy wishes for a brief second to be Lilian. She has all her life spread before her and the hindsight of her sister's mistakes. Lilian told her not to marry Samuel, but would she listen? To Sissy he was brooding and powerful, everything manly and he made her feel safe. Her father made her feel the same, but Sissy soon found out Samuel is everything her father wasn't. Her father was a real man who knew how to treat a woman. When he came home from work, he chatted about his day, sharing anecdotes and funny stories at teatime. He never went to the pub except on a weekend because he liked to spend his evenings at home with his family. He took some ribbing about it, but he didn't care one jot because he was a real man. But her father can't save her now.

"I'm talking to you," Samuel says combing his wet hair in the mantle mirror.

She stops dishing up the stew she made this morning to simmer to perfection in the range all day.

"I know you work hard, love. I don't often get a minute, but I can't really slam the door in the face of my own mother and sister."

She fusses with the cutlery as she awaits his response.

"I don't often get a minute," he mimics with a high-pitched tone, "You should try swapping lives for a day or two, that'd give you a taste of proper work. See how you would like it when your back's bent double and your hands are claws you need to unravel at the end of a shift because you've been holding and swinging a pick for twelve hours."

Sissy has never been sure why she lives in fear of her husband as she does. He's never laid a hand on her unlike some of the women on the row who have a catalogue of excuses prepared to explain the reason for their latest bruise. They prefer to live in a fantasy world even though they live on top of one another and the rest of the street can hear all the comings and goings. She doesn't blame them; they must do whatever they need to get through each day.

Samuel has his reputation to think of so he's far subtler about controlling his wife; devious some might call it. But Sissy has made her own bed to lie in, nobody forced her to marry him.

She often indulges in a daydream of packing her bags and leaving a note behind the mantle clock for him to come home to. She imagines his face when he walks around the door in his underwear and his wife's nowhere to be seen. It makes her smile. Sometimes her daydreaming goes to darker places where she slips something nasty in his tea or on worse days, pinning him up against the wall by his throat. If only she had the strength of mind and body. It's the steady drip, drip, drip effect of constant belittling and undermining that takes her to these places. At least she hopes so, she hopes she isn't evil.

Only half an hour to go before he's out the door again. This gives him just enough time to gobble down a supper in minutes that took hours to make and then read the paper. They empty the bath outside the door then she calls the boys down to eat their supper.

They come running down the stairs, Harry the eldest first, fair-haired and blue-eyed like his father then Jack, darker skinned like her. If his father has any affection for anyone it's for Harry, his firstborn, but not so much that Harry doesn't have the same sense of trepidation as his mother and brother. His father's unpredictability means they can be laughing at a joke with him one minute then listening to him rant the next. Samuel revels in the thrill of keeping them on tenterhooks, always needing to second-guess his mood. She can tell he's come home if she nips out just by the atmosphere on entering the house. It's as though he casts an evil spell on what should be the sanctity of home.

Tonight, Sissy stares through the window after Samuel leaves to meet his cronies at the *Billet*. She often catches herself standing still, her thoughts in a knot. She raises the sash a little to let in the fresh air so she can breathe properly again.

Her mind wanders back to the plan now he's gone, the one which is keeping her going through each day. The plan which has her staring toward the ceiling in the blackness of the bedroom, whilst she listens to her husband snoring. She twirls her plait between her fingers as she lays there knowing she won't need to suffer this turmoil for much longer.

It was all Lilian's idea—they've talked and talked about it for weeks, and now Sissy can't stop thinking about the future. Lilian is coming to her sister's rescue. They've thought of every setback they can imagine and have come too far now to let anything stand in their way.

After five long, miserable years, the worm is about to turn.

Chapter 7

1886—Annalise

The accolades crowd the wall above the piano. There are nine certificates presented to Emmanuel Goldsmith for excellence in so many instruments including his voice. They're all written in beautiful script by his many tutors over the years. Emmanuelle Goldsmith must surely be a musical genius.

Unfortunately, I'm unable to follow suit. Piano lessons alone are proving difficult for me to master.

Fifteen months I've been coming here every Wednesday evening to Mr Greenacre's snug little study. His wife is in the kitchen with their five children around the table during the two-hour lesson. Without fail they come into the hallway to greet me on arrival, and I must have tea before I leave. How cheerful and lively this house is, full of music and laughter. I often wish I lived in a house just like it but as wonderful as mama and papa are, it would need siblings to complete the picture.

"I know you have every faith in my progress, Mr Greenacre but I'm mediocre at best. When I watch you play it's as if your hands dance across the keyboard, but my own hands aren't anywhere near as adept. They're far too small for a start."

I hold them up to demonstrate my point and he chuckles. I join him and it helps soothe my exasperation at my inadequacies. How I've tried to be a piano player, I can never be accused of not giving it my best shot.

"I confess I've been having the same thoughts of late, my dear. Forgive me, I feel somewhat guilty for wasting your father's money when the improvement since you started is so slight."

I raise my eyebrows at his comment.

"Well, wasting might be too strong a word but let us try something different tonight, just for fun."

Staring up at him I see his eyes twinkling behind his glasses. I smile, thinking I must continue to come here because this lesson is the highlight of my week. We have become friends and I see so little of papa he helps to fill the void.

We became friends unexpectedly when, frustrated at my lack of musical talent one teatime, I suddenly burst into tears which is quite unlike me. Without a word Mr Greenacre handed me his huge handkerchief and guided me to the chair by the fireside. I sat sniffling a moment whilst he chewed on the end of his unlit pipe. He was trying to stop because Mrs Greenacre hated the smell so that way, he could still enjoy the flavour … and a quiet life he told me.

"I'm sorry," I said, "I'm not quite myself today. Papa hasn't been home much of late, and mama seems quiet and distracted. It can be quite lonely at Hardcastle, and sometimes I don't always feel I belong there, which I know is silly of me. I wish the house were smaller like this for a start," I sighed and dabbed my tears before I looked at him, "You must think me very ungrateful."

Placing his pipe back on the rack he shook his head.

"Ah, I see, then it seems you and I have a great deal in common, Miss Whitworth. I know something of feeling like I don't belong."

I sat back in the chair wondering what he was referring to. To my mind he had a loving wife and family in a home which almost sang with fun and laughter.

"I'm not sure what you mean," I said.

He glanced at his pocket watch to be sure we had time for a story.

"Well, my dear, I know it might be hard for you to believe but I had a very upsetting time before I came to live here."

He tilted his head to one side as he looked at me. I wondered if he wasn't sure if he should go on, but perhaps my tearstained face gave him the answer.

"I know you think I live a perfect life in this little house but to live here I had to pay a price. I had to turn my back on my old life and my faith. I have made myself an outcast."

"An outcast?" I asked. Surely this calm, gentle man could never be such a person.

"My family have disowned me. You see, I fell in love, and I had to make a choice. Sometimes, though not so often nowadays, I think I have lost my place in the world. So, I can understand how you feel, my dear."

Frowning, I shook my head at him.

"But you seem so happy with your life," I said.

His smile was kindly.

"Yes, I am, very happy and one day you will be too. You're at an age where life starts to present adult challenges, your mind is full of questions. This lessens over time when you find out who you are. You're old for your years but you can't possibly know who you are at sixteen so you mustn't be so hard on yourself. You mustn't rush things."

He glanced at the certificates.

"Did you not ever wonder about the names on the certificates? He continued before I could answer:

"You know me as Maxwell Greenacre, but this isn't my real name. I created Maxwell Greenacre so my wife's family would accept me. I am Emmanuel Goldman. I can see him search the past through rheumy eyes.

"When I was boy my friends called me Manny. Ah, happy days. Do you know…," then suddenly, as if remembering where he was, he stopped and then resumed, eyes clear and sharp again.

"I will always keep my faith in my heart and in private but to marry Mrs Greenacre I had to become someone else. I don't know if I have fooled everybody, but I believe I have been accepted."

I couldn't really understand why he had to make a choice. I was upset by the thought of the choice he had to make and I was disappointed in myself for making a mountain out of a molehill.

I will always be grateful to Mr Greenacre for trying to help me in that moment. To this day I keep his secret.

"So," he says now, "today we will try different tactics to coax that pianist from out of you. Today I will sing, he proclaimed, throwing his hands in the air, whilst you play. I'm thinking it might be that you're self-conscious when I'm watching you. You possess a gift many of my students do not have—the gift of musicality. So have faith in yourself. Now, we shall play the piece you have been practicing, *The Holly and the Ivy*. Are you ready?"

I nod, my fingers poised on the keyboard. I'm willing to give anything a try.

"After three. One, two, three."

How lovely his voice is I think as he sings the first line. My fingers trace the melody and he's right, I'm freer, less wooden without his gaze upon me. I ease into the notes I know off by heart now and allow myself to think of nothing else but the music. After a few bars I begin to sing along too, this is more like it. Musicality, musicality I've been bestowed the gift of musicality, I think, my eyes closed, my head moving from side to side in time with the words and music.

As the last note of the hymn floats away, my eyes remain closed until the very last hum has left the room never to return. I feel renewed, hopeful we might continue with our lessons at least.

When I finally open them, he is staring at me with tears in his eyes, a bright glow about his cheeks. How pleased I am with him for his idea and for him allowing me the freedom to turn a corner.

"Well, Miss Whitworth, Annalise," he says, "I am quite correct in my thinking it seems. Your piano playing is improved but I think your father's money has indeed been wasted on piano lessons."

My mouth drops, the wind taken from my sails by such a harsh assessment when I was so euphoric only a second ago. I swallow down the tears, closing the piano lid.

"No, no, please do not be disheartened," he says, his hand touching my arm.

"Today we have made a far more important discovery. A significant one."

"I don't know what you mean," I say and mean it. I am completely perplexed.

"I lost myself in the music the way you asked, and I felt it deep within my heart. I could hear the difference myself."

Taking both my hands in his Mr Greenacre lifts me from the piano stool to hold me at arm's length, a broad smile cracking his face.

"Never fear, we are to go on a new adventure together which starts this very day. First, I must speak to your father but when he hears what I have just heard he will surely agree with my assessment."

Shaking my head, I can't help but be infected by the happy look on his face. He has good news I know it and my own face cracks with a smile.

"My dearest girl, I can't comprehend it," he says, "I am utterly bewitched. Has nobody in all your life never told you that you have been blessed with nothing less than the voice of an angel?"

Chapter 8

1886 - Annalise

Mama is having a lie down before dinner. She's taken to doing this a lot of late. Is she sick I wonder, are she and papa hiding something from me? I miss her; even when she's in the room, I miss her. Our chats are stilted, as though she's trying too hard to make conversation, so I won't suspect something is wrong.

Miss Lewis, my governess has left our service now leaving me limited option for conversation until papa comes home. She was my governess for ten years and I used to enjoy listening to stories of her childhood in Ireland. By comparison, my childhood has been so isolated I can't think of one interesting tale to tell. I try not to be ungrateful, but life at Hardcastle can be dull sometimes.

When Miss Lewis was packing her case, she told me she would prefer to be married rather than take her new position in Kent. She said it didn't matter about her speaking openly any longer because she was leaving, and anyway I was a young woman now.

"I had chance to marry the boy next door when I was seventeen, Annalise, but I decided to spread my wings before they were clipped," she said joining me to sit on edge of her bed, "I think I may have clipped them myself in the end. Sadly, Michael went on to marry another girl from the village."

I stared at her face in profile thinking how beautiful she was with her sandy coloured hair, but Michael can't have loved her if he married somebody else.

I felt I must console her though I knew the chance of meeting someone to marry was limited as a governess.

"There will be others I'm sure of it, Miss Lewis, you're far too pretty to be an old maid," I said.

Throwing her head back she laughed so loudly I was startled. It was the first time I'd heard the sound of her laughter in ten whole years I realised. She seemed like a young girl, yet she told me she was almost twenty-nine. How strange she wasn't many years older than me when she came to work here.

"All I will say to you before I leave, my dear, is don't close the door to opportunity too hastily. You must learn by my mistakes."

Now Miss Lewis has taken charge of a boy and two girls and Kent seems so very far away. We've written to each other but it's not the same and I've come to accept I may never see her again.

Since her departure I've even taken to coming down early to chat to Doris whilst she lights the fire. I'm not sure if she welcomes the intrusion into her domestic routine so I may have to reconsider. My weekly visits to see Mr and Mrs Greenacre in their cosy terraced house in the east of the city seem to be taking longer to come around.

"Darling," mama says bustling into the drawing room, "I lost track of time, you should have woken me, papa is due any minute. I have a surprise for you; we have a visitor after dinner this evening."

A visitor? It's a long time since we've had company. I think the last people who came were Mr and Mrs Abbey. Mr Abbey works for papa as his righthand man as he calls him, but I ate separately as they thought I would have been bored with talk of business.

"Oh, please don't keep me in suspense, mama, who is coming to see us."

Her blonde hair is styled differently after her nap. She has curls about her forehead and ears making her face somehow look softer. Perhaps Miss Pawson, mama's lady's maid has persuaded her to try something new as I've never seen her with any other hairstyle than a simple low bun. Mama smiles playfully, her eyes dancing and she looks so lovely.

"I'm sure you'll be delighted to find out Mr Greenacre is coming to see us tonight; I know how fond you are of him. I'll be glad to finally meet him in person."

Mr Greenacre? What a lovely surprise indeed. I wonder what he could be coming to discuss. Oh dear, I think suddenly, I hope he doesn't want to end my singing lessons, I know I'll go quite mad if this is the case.

"Do you know why he's coming to see us?" I ask.

"I have no idea. He asked to see your papa and so it was arranged. Papa also knew you'd be pleased to see him."

Dear papa, he waits an hour longer than is necessary to collect me after my lesson because he knows I like to take tea with Mr Greenacre and his family. I spin out my time away from Hardcastle because once that door closes behind me, I know there will be a long week ahead.

Mama glances at her hair in the mirror of the sideboard as we hear the slam of papa's carriage door.

"Your hair suits you like that, mama, you should wear it like that all the time," I tell her.

She seems more herself after her nap. Twiddling a curl into place at the nape of her neck she smiles at my reflection.

"Oh, Pawson hasn't time to be faffing with my hair every day," she laughs, "She's quite busy enough."

The parlour door opens, and papa stands looking between us both.

"Here are my girls," he says, striding across the room to kiss mama's cheek first as he does every evening. Tonight though, he pauses to peer at her more closely.

"Your hair is different, Clara. I like it, don't you, Annalise?" he asks, wandering to the settee and stooping to kiss my forehead.

The room is brighter already, papa's homecoming is the highlight of our day. Mama says he brings the sunshine in, and I think that's a perfect description.

I haven't time to answer as Cockcroft announces supper is ready a little earlier than usual. Papa says there's no time to change, so mama and I saunter to the dining room arm in arm. The candelabra is lit, the wine open and waiting as we sit at one end of our overly long dining table. It's far too big for the three of us. Papa eventually takes his seat at the head of the table, and then mama and I settle ourselves in the seats either side of him.

I'm bursting to ask the question and don't waste any time.

"Do you know why Mr Greenacre is coming this evening, papa," I ask as Cockcroft serves our soup.

Papa takes a sip of wine and replaces his glass on the silver coaster with an odd expression on his face.

"I do know, yes, but I refuse to spoil the surprise for you both. His visit is irregular, but I assure you there is nothing to worry about; quite the opposite in fact."

Mama and I exchange glances, raising our eyebrows at one another. This evening is proving to be irregular in so many ways already.

"It's nice to come home earlier for a change," papa says, touching our hands briefly, "I'm sorry, I realise leaving work later seems to have become a habit but there's so much to be done. I was saying as much to Mr Abbey and Stevie in our meeting earlier today."

"It's nice to have you home early, my dear," mama says as they share a smile.

My parents are so different yet so matched. They complement one another—papa being lively and outgoing whilst mama is gentle and kind. I often catch them sharing brief kisses and holding hands. I truly hope to have a marriage like theirs one day but how I will ever meet anyone is beyond me. If I'm not careful I'll end up an old maid like Miss Lewis. There was talk of a summer ball last year, but it never happened and I was so disappointed.

After supper we retire to the drawing room to await Mr Greenacre's arrival. Papa has a glass of brandy whilst mama enjoys a small glass of port. I glance impatiently at the clock on the mantle all the while we chat wishing the time away.

Finally, I hear horse's hooves on gravel followed by voices in the hallway as mama and papa smile my way enjoying my excitement.

"Mr Greenacre to see you sir," Cockcroft announces.

Papa gets to his feet, as I sit back down in my seat as is only proper though I can't help but fidget. Mr Greenacre looks a little ill at ease in this new environment, but I'm so pleased to see my music teacher's friendly face.

"Good evening, Greenacre, a pleasure to see you. Thank you for coming on this cold night and welcome," papa says shaking his hand, "I don't believe you've met my wife before."

"How do you do, Mr Greenacre," mama says inclining her head.

"It is a great pleasure to finally meet you, Mrs Whitworth," he says taking mama's hand in his large palm," he does the same to me, saying, "Miss Whitworth."

"How nice to see you and so unexpectedly, Mr Greenacre," I say smiling up at him, part pleasantry and part question.

Papa shows him to the seat at the other end of the settee where I'm seated. He accepts a brandy, sitting back with a sigh and turns his head my way.

"Well, my dear, I'm sure you've been waiting impatiently to find out why I'm here," he says.

"Yes, I have rather but patience is a virtue as you tell me."

He lets out a small chuckle then looks between my parents.

"Firstly, may I say what a fine young lady you have raised in Annalise, Mr and Mrs Whitworth. She is a credit to you both," he says.

Mama's cheeks turn pinkish, and father inclines his head at the compliment saying, "Thank you, of course we are very proud of our daughter."

Mr Greenacre shuffles forward in his seat as I sit all ears.

"So, I've come this evening to discuss an opportunity; an opportunity for Annalise which I feel compelled to bring to your notice."

Papa's half-smile confirms he knows what is about to be disclosed.

We're all looking at Mr Greenacre and he has our full attention.

"I have already spoken to your husband, Mrs Whitworth about a former colleague of mine in London."

Mr Greenacre pauses, taking in our expressions in turn.

"I must apologise for the secrecy, Mrs Whitworth, but it was important not to raise hopes until

60

we had an unbiased and expert opinion. My colleague and I are in full agreement."

"I see," mama says, glancing at papa with a wry smile, "So, tell me Mr Greenacre, what has been deduced from your covert conversations."

My teacher takes a swig of his brandy as though to settle his nerves.

"Well, we agree your daughter has a natural talent, a gift if you will. If you recall, some two years ago I suggested Annalise change her musical instrument lessons from piano to voice and she was in agreement. I confess when I first heard her singing voice I was astonished, the mezzo soprano tones were quite perfect, the best I have ever heard in one so young. However, I knew her voice would change with age, and it certainly has … but only for the better."

Papa is positively glowing, his face lit up like a sunbeam.

"What Mr Greenacre is saying my darling, is that you have quite an extraordinary talent. I don't profess to be an expert in these matters but, I heard it with my own ears."

My brow knits as I shake my head.

"But how, papa. You have never attended my singing lessons."

Papa looks at Mr Greenacre, saying, "Shall I elaborate whilst you enjoy your brandy, my friend?"

Mr Greenacre nods, nestling into his seat, all set to listen to papa tell a tale he already knows.

"Mr Greenacre's friend, Mr Bamford is eminent in his field with the latest voice recording instruments. However, we thought you would be too self-conscious,

Annalise if you knew your singing was being recorded. So, Mr Bamford set up the equipment discreetly out of sight in Mr Greenacre's music room."

Mama and I start speaking at the same time, as papa holds up his hands in defence.

"I know, I know, and we're sorry for being so underhand, genuinely."

The room falls quiet a moment with only the sound of the wind and the crackling of the fire in the background. When I finally hear mama's voice it sounds strange.

"So, Garrison I must understand, what are you saying exactly?" she asks, standing to walk to the fireplace.

There's no humour about her face as she places one hand on the mantle, the other to her throat as if she's struggling for breath.

"I'm saying, Clara that *The Royal Opera* house in London would like Annalise to pay them a visit at our earliest convenience," papa says, walking to take both her hands in his.

"Mr Bamford has contacts there and…" but mama isn't listening any longer, swiftly snatching her hands away from his grasp before she storms out of the room.

I don't know which one of us is more surprised. I've never witnessed such drama, and from mama of all people.

Chapter 9

1886 – Sissy & Lilian

No, mam, marriage isn't all roses and chocolates, Sissy thinks but neither is it meant to be despair and misery. She bites her tongue now deciding not to mention the fact she would have no idea about despair and misery because her father was a different kettle of fish altogether to Samuel.

"The boys are grown, you should be spending more time together not pushing him away," her mother says, "what I wouldn't give to be able grow old with your father. He was taken from me too young."

Not for the first time Sissy rues the day she decided to keep her mother in the dark about her marriage, forever playing the situation down. She didn't want her to worry, but now with the boys out of the house more, life is becoming stifling. Sissy is struggling to keep her house of cards standing and many a day thinks she's on her way to doing something drastic. What the drastic thing could be she can't be sure.

How she wishes Samuel would just leave her but she knows he never will because if he left, he'd miss out on his daily dose of chipping away at her self-confidence. He needs it like a pill; it makes him feel better, feel stronger. It's sustenance for his ego. If he upped and left, it would give her the push she needed, she'd have no choice then but to find her own way in the world.

But Sissy has started to believe her husband. Her self-confidence has long since fled out the door because she's getting older, getting flabbier no matter how much she tries to keep her figure. Age is not being kind to her. Sometimes she stares at her reflection in the full-length mirror of the wardrobe and thinks she could almost be mistaken for Lilian's mother. Is it because she's bitter she wonders; is it corroding her from within?

She decides to change the subject with her mother before she loses her reason.

"Have you seen our Lilian?"

Somehow, she always has to ask, more from curiosity than concern for her sister's welfare.

Her mother puts down her sandwich and dabs at the corners of her mouth with her napkin. They're sitting at the kitchen table, but they may as well be sitting in a regal dining room decked with lace doyleys and delicate cups and saucers. The line in the yard is already strewn with washing, it being a Monday and a fine spring day. Her mother makes keeping house seem so effortless.

"I hadn't seen her until I called at the cottage last week. You know how elusive your little sister can be."

Elusive is not the word, wild is better, Sissy thinks. She has no intention of settling down with Stevie, she's only stringing him along for her own ends, poor lad.

Lilian had been her ticket to leaving Samuel. Their plan was airtight after a house came up for rent on Bright Eye Lane: they were going to move in together and Lilian was going to rescue her sister from the hell she was living.

Lilian was working in the canteen at Whitworth's, and she was going to get Sissy a job so they could afford the rent. Mr Whitworth would be on board, she said. Sissy was squirreling the odd tuppence away here and there from the housekeeping when she could cut a few corners and she was allowing herself to become excited. It was all agreed.

Then the Friday before they were due to sign up for the rent, Lilian snuck in the back door and plonked herself down at the table. She knew Sissy would be on her own and she listened to her sister telling her about what she planned to write in the 'Dear John' note for Samuel. Something simple and straight to the point would be best she thought.

"I'd like to give him a piece of my mind but then I don't want to rattle him, so he comes all guns blazing to Bright Eye Lane, we ..."

"I can't do it, Sissy," Lilian said.

Just like that, "I can't do it, Sissy."

Sissy stared at her thinking she'd misheard. Lilian's hair was coming loose around her ears, and she'd scraped it back with water somehow making it look even more of a mess.

"Are you having a laugh, Lily?" Sissy asked.

Lilian glanced up at her sister and shook her head. Sissy towered over her as she stood with the teapot in her hand.

"Look, I don't expect you to understand," Lilian said, "you're all domesticated, a little housewife and

Bright Eye Lane would suit you down to the ground. But I'm not like you. I've never lived with anybody else since mam and now I've left the street, I can't go back to all that. Washing nets and scrubbing front steps just isn't for me, Sis."

Sissy's chest was pounding, blood rushing around her head so she felt like Lilian was speaking underwater. Her own sister had pushed her off a cliff. Sissy didn't move, her only thought was to convince Lilian it would be fine.

"You won't have to wash nets and such, I'll do all that. All you have to do is pay half the rent. It's not just me, it's the boys, Lilian, they're starting to notice more now their older. Please, love, we can do it together."

Lilian played with a thread on her dress. It was clean but that's about all to be said for it, an iron had never been near it. Her little toe was peering up at Sissy from her stockings.

Lilian dropped her head back.

"Don't you think I haven't given it plenty of thought? I've been laid awake worrying about it, but I can't go back to that life. I love living in the little cottage on my own. Yes, Stevie calls round most days but then he goes home, and I like that, he does too, I think. You say you'll do everything, but you'll soon come to resent me and then the bickering will start, then the rowing. It wouldn't work in the long run."

Sissy thought she might be sick. All her hopes and dreams were coming crashing around her ears, and she couldn't stand it. To get up tomorrow and know she was still trapped with no end in sight, it was too much.

"It's not just about your life, Lilian, it's about me too and your nephews. I'm desperate, I'll do anything to get out of here so there won't be any rowing from me, you mark my words."

Lilian dropped her head onto her forearms resting on the table. She was expecting to hear all these arguments from her sister, but she'd made up her mind. Sissy began to cry quietly which tweaked her conscience but still she couldn't say yes.

It was too much to give up. Mr Whitworth saw her right, the job in the canteen was more of a cover story than anything else and she really didn't need much.

"What happened to you, Lilian?" Sissy asked, turning to stare out into the back yard, "You don't seem normal any longer. When we were growing up you were a tomboy, but you seemed normal. We had the same dreams for the future, or so I thought."

Lilian tutted and pulled at the thread on her skirt so much a tiny hole appeared.

"I never had your aspirations, Sissy, we never had the discussion, but I didn't want what you wanted."

Sissy puts the teapot down because she'd like to smash it against the wall. She's startled when Lilian raises her head to stare her straight in the eye.

"And then … and then of course there was … the baby."

She chose the words carefully. They'd never spoken of the baby before. She wasn't sure if that was deliberate or not, but they hadn't.

But either way Lilian had held the trump card all along.

Sissy flopped down in the chair like a ragdoll with all the stuffing pulled from her by her sister.

She was beaten.

Chapter 10

1892—Annalise

Mama's face creases as she draws me quickly into her embrace. The feel of velvet against my cheek is soothing and I close my eyes to it as I breathe in the scent of my mother. She always smells the same and this is one of the comforts I shall miss.

"We find ourselves at the end of an era, Annalise," she says, sniffing slightly, "Are you quite sure you have everything you need before I get on the train?"

Touching her cheek, I smile at her dear face reddened and sullied with tears.

"Please don't worry, mama, I'm in good hands with Mr Bamford. You're a hard act to follow but he will do his best, I'm sure. I'll see you on Tuesday."

Her shoulders drop.

"Well until Tuesday then, my dear," she says scrabbling for a clean handkerchief in her handbag.

She nods at Mr Elston, the stationmaster who's loitering a discreet distance from us, allowing us some privacy. He dutifully loads her large case and paraphernalia into the carriage, an expert at the task after so many years. Mr Elston is only one of the many stationmasters we've come to know by name.

Mama sits in the window seat of the carriage looking like a little girl lost; it's as though she might

69

never see me again. I reach for her hand as the whistle blows then run alongside bidding her farewell as she's slowly swept away. Too soon I lose her in a cloud of steam as the train leaves Kings Cross station, and I picture her weeping into her handkerchief once again.

Five years is a long time to be my constant companion. Trotting towards Mr Bamford who's been waiting patiently for me under the station clock, I think how cross mama was with papa for keeping her in the dark about his plan for my future.

Mr Greenacre left us shortly after mama flounced from the room. I'm sure now papa thought he would convince her it was the right path for me because he told Mr Greenacre he would see him soon before he left us.

Papa said we could resume the discussion tomorrow and I made my way to bed. But when I was brushing my hair, I heard mama going back downstairs. Somehow, I couldn't help but follow her to eavesdrop at the parlour door. It was so very unlike me but then the evening had been unlike any other.

"Did either of you think for one moment about asking my opinion before raising Annalise's hopes? I can't believe this is what you would want for our daughter Garrison: a life on the stage indeed. It will ruin her prospects."

Mama paused as if contemplating further reasons this was a terrible idea.

"It will be me who will need to accompany her to London It will be a significant upheaval not just to our daughter's life but to all our lives," she said.

Her voice sounded odd; it was raised slightly, and I'd never heard her raise her voice before.

"My dear Clara, this is the Royal Opera House, we are talking about, not some penny-ha'penny music hall. Annelise will be held in the highest regard by the whole of London society, mark my words. If she fulfils her potential, Mr Greenacre said she will sing before the Prince of Wales."

Mama had nothing to say to that proclamation, though I was astonished, but papa clearly thought she needed more convincing.

He went on, "Surely you understand we had to find out first if her voice is good enough to pursue singing as a career. Perhaps you're right, I've been swept up in all the excitement and I wanted you both to share in it too. Whether I told you first or not, however, we couldn't have let her miss out on this opportunity. She had to try at least. What kind of resentment would it breed to deny her the pursuit of her talent? Mr Bamford said he had never heard such a voice. "Believe me, Mr Whitworth, he said, I have heard some wonderful voices in my time but never one of such a natural quality. Your daughter barely needs to try to sing. This is rare, so very rare." We must think of our daughter's future, Clara."

I could hear mama's sigh even through the barrier of the door.

"But I like my simple life here at Hardcastle. I'm a hearth and home person, you know this more than anybody."

"Are you really, dear? You don't seem to be yourself of late. I think perhaps you're a little bored. In any case, you're jumping ahead. There are many bridges to be crossed before anything can be confirmed. Stage fright may cripple Analise, or she may be homesick. Don't you think it would be better to take one step at a time before we make a final decision?" he lowered his voice, "I apologise for not speaking to you first, Clara, I understand now this was impetuous of me."

The room fell silent.

"Fine, I'll go to London with her for the meeting and we'll take it from there," she said, but not ungraciously.

Their voices went to whispers, and I ran back upstairs more than happy with the plan.

So, it was all agreed. The following week we took the train to London and papa accompanied us. That in itself was an adventure as I'd never been away from Hardcastle overnight let alone been to London.

Mr Bamford met us off the train and we took a carriage to Bow Street. When I set eyes on the pale stone portico of the Royal Opera House that first time I was awestruck. Covent Garden was a hive of activity as we alighted the carriage and I stood and watched hordes of people going about their business. I was invisible to them, but they were all I could see.

Oh, the wonder of seeing the magnificent pillars, the glass dome, the auditorium for the very first time as we followed Mr Bamford into the building. The memory will stay with me always.

After a tour of the opera house, we met with Mr Francis, the musical director, in a small side room adjacent to the rehearsal studio. It wasn't as grand as I might have imagined but I didn't care because I was so excited to just be a part of it all.

However, he never once asked me to sing. I was glad when papa questioned this on our way out, realising then he was as perplexed as I was.

"All in good time, Mr Whitworth," Mr Francis said, shaking papa's hand "I think you should enjoy the city this weekend, there's no rush and I would hate to scare our young prodigy away."

He smiled warmly at me, and I decided I liked him immediately.

He asked if mama would bring me down once a week. She agreed but it was clear to me at least she was hesitant. This was a big commitment, but papa looked overjoyed when she agreed.

So, every Wednesday mama and I travelled down to London on the early train and returned home late in the evening.

That first Wednesday she heard me sing backstage at the opera house for the very first time. After only two bars of the melody, I could see her eyes were wide and misted and I was reminded of Mr Greenacre's expression when I first sang for him.

"Annalise, my darling, I wish I had heard you sing before because now I understand what all the fuss is about," she said when I'd finished, "I cannot believe that I, your own mother hasn't heard you sing properly before. A little humming yes but never a song. Was I living too much in my own mind I wonder. I feel positively neglectful."

We all laughed. I told her I'd never felt in the least bit neglected, but I had come to wonder why we'd never thought to at least have little singalong of some description at Hardcastle.

    Mr Francis didn't appear to be in any rush for me to stand on the stage of the opera house much less sing on it. He said there was much work to be done and singing was just a part of it. There was so much I didn't know. I needed to be able to read music, to learn some stagecraft and most importantly and worryingly, I would need to learn German, French and Italian.

    When I queried why I couldn't sing in English Mr Francis simply rolled his eyes and sighed: "Opera is beauty, Miss Whitworth, and its language is beautiful too; but never fear, we shall make a silk purse of you yet."

    I felt a little admonished, but underneath his patronising glance I sensed it was all part of his grand plan for me.

    The training went on for six months. It was monotonous and at times painful on my throat. I was managing the music and vocal tuition well and the language classes were also progressing. I found Italian easier than the French and German and Mr Francis mentioned starting out with something about cavaliers. But the stage classes with Miss De Vries weren't going so well. I was terribly shy, feeling very unnatural acting out parts. I could sense how uncomfortable and gauche I must look and thought that if I could actually be allowed to sing a song – aria Mr Francis would correct – then it would be easier.

    Then one Wednesday just before Christmas I asked the question: could I see how my voice sounded from the stage? Mr Bamford and Mr Francis looked at one another and smiled. I smiled too; I was ready. I had been rehearsing a piece privately for a while on my walks around the gardens at home. It was time for me to take the next step.

On Wednesday 20th December, mama, papa and I travelled down together for the day to London, accompanied by Mr and Mrs Greenacre.

As I paced the worn wooden boards of the rehearsal studio, I asked myself if I was nervous. I went up and down my scales in preparation and thought of the small group waiting for me with heightened anticipation. I thought of them positioned in their front seats next to the stage, all their dreams for my future floating around their minds.

But I wasn't nervous. I wondered if the nerves might appear when I stood on the vast stage or when I heard the orchestra play the opening notes of *Inneggiamo* from my new favourite: *Cavalleria Rusticana*. The first note came and went. And when I looked into the eyes of Mr Greenacre, and I recalled our special day in his little study two years before I simply fell headfirst into the music.

For this and so many other things I shall always remain eternally grateful to my dear friend, Mr Emmanuelle Goldsmith.

Chapter 11
1892 - Annalise

Life is now a merry go round of rehearsals and train journeys to and from Yorkshire. Mama is still accompanying me to London and papa is always keen to hear every detail of our day on return.

I was allowed to join the chorus for the company's last production *Gotterdammerung*— a small role in act two which Mr Francis said would give me some valuable experience of being in front of an audience, adding snippily, "So we can see how that pretty voice of yours holds up."

I take in the splendour of the hotel Mr Bamford has chosen for us for afternoon tea. Papa will simply be thrilled to hear about this little gem when I describe the Carrera marble floors, the gold-leaf light fittings, the opulent fireplaces permanently blazing up the chimney back, yet I haven't seen anybody stoking them. It all seems to happen as if by magic.

"Mrs Whitworth, I fear I have an ulterior motive for bringing you to the *Hotel Cecil* today," Mr Bamford says.

Mama's mouth tightens into a line in preparation for yet another revelation. They have become a regular occurrence.

"I see," she says a hand straying to her throat.

Though her voice is calm, her mind is far from it; I know her.

"Yes, I was wondering if you would consider staying here from say Thursdays until Sundays?" Mr Bamford asks, "Annalise has made wonderful progress, beyond our expectations but must be allowed to focus entirely on her studies if she is to achieve her full potential."

Mother doesn't respond immediately and nervous of the silence Mr Bamford continues, "You and Annalise would be well looked after, the manager here is a personal friend of mine. This would be your home from home."

Mama dabs at the corner of her mouth and sits back in her chair.

"I think I know where my home is Mr Bamford, and what is best for me and my daughter."

He has tipped the balance so she can no longer hide her irritation. The spring sunshine flooding the conservatory windows highlights the tired folds of her eyes. I've been too preoccupied to notice the toll travelling has taken on her.

"I'm sorry, mama, I hadn't realised how exhausting life has been for you now that we're travelling here twice weekly for rehearsals," I say, taking her hand, "Forgive me."

She sits up straight, smiling my way but this doesn't succeed in making her look any less weary.

"My darling, you have nothing to reproach yourself for. The opera world is taking you on an exciting adventure which I am more than happy to share with you," she turns to Mr Bamford, "However, I do have a husband and a life in Yorkshire, so I find myself in a quandary, Mr Bamford."

He has no idea about the responsibilities of a family; he can live and breathe his work without a care. His suit is not the finest, his grey hair not the tidiest because he has no time for vanity. His clients are his family and his sole priority, anything else seems a bother to him.

"Is Mr Whitworth still as keen for Annalise to make a name for herself in the capital?" he asks.

Taking a dainty sip of her tea mama nods, "He is indeed but very preoccupied with work. Only my own guilt stands in the way."

"I do understand. We have overlooked that your life has been upended and changed beyond recognition. Annalise has the naivety of youth as a defence whilst I have no such excuse."

He bows his head. He looks so forlorn I feel I must interject.

"Well, perhaps we are jumping ahead. My opening night is not until Saturday, and we have no idea how I will be received until then. I think perhaps we should delay any decision making until afterwards. What do you think, mama?"

"Opening night? She asks, enunciating each syllable as if the meaning might change.

Mr Bamford turns to my mother. She turns her head now, averting her attention from me to my agent with a raised eyebrow.

"Mrs Whitworth, you and your husband have created a remarkable young lady, far more mature than her years. How proud you must be."

*

Mr Bamford is being quite overbearing.

"After much deliberation I think this the best choice," he tells mama, his voice slightly raised, "White and pastels are too childlike and black too funereal, too austere. Red is the perfect colour. Don't you agree it complements her dark hair and complexion."

Mama holds a hand to her forehead, cheeks flushing pink. They're behaving as though I'm not in the room.

"And I still think you should have told me the colour dress my young daughter would be wearing for her opening night. You billed the unveiling of the dress as a surprise and now I find myself wondering if it was a ploy, Mr Bamford. She has barely turned eighteen, I dread to think what my husband with make of it!"

Closing my eyes, I skulk away from the heated debate. Bickering seems to have become a regular occurrence between my mother and agent, each with their own agenda. I must remind myself they both have my best interests at heart.

Dabbing my nose with powder I smooth my already perfect hair in the reflection of the mirror. There's no longer a smattering of freckles on my nose; I barely recognise myself.

"It's not too late to slow things down, Annalise. It's never too late, remember this."

I recall what papa said to me when we were alone the other night. My face flew in his direction; what an odd thing for him to say when up until then he'd been nothing but encouraging.

Mama had retired for the night, and we were sitting by the lowering fire enjoying a rare moment alone.

"What are you saying, papa?" I asked, "Do you think I should?"

Swirling the brandy in his glass he studied my face for a while. I could hear the ticking of the grandfather clock from the hallway.

"The question my dear, sweet daughter is, are you happy?"

"Oh yes, I feel I was born to be an opera singer."

I replied without hesitation because it's true, something I feel in my heart, in my bones even. When I sing, I become another person and one I like very much.

Setting down his brandy he took the few steps to sit beside me and took my hand.

"Then this is all I need to hear. I was concerned you may have been pushed down a path that wasn't of your choosing. Sometimes it can be hard to get out of a situation once you're in it. You've convinced me we're doing the right thing and you're not getting carried along on a wave."

I gripped his hand tightly.

"I thought you were having second thoughts, papa or perhaps knew something I didn't," I said.

Relief flooded me when I knew that wasn't the case, another sign of my commitment.

"Now you must do what you must do to ensure your success. This is the difference between the many and the few; many have talent, but few are prepared to make the sacrifices success demands and they fall short of their maximum potential."

So, I ask myself the question: will wearing red compromise my own personal boundaries? The answer is a resounding no.

The noise outside the dressing room grows steadily louder. My anticipation grows in tandem, but time seems to have slowed.

There's a brisk rap on the door and Elizabeth Gilbert appears in her finery. Elizabeth never fails to point out that the 'g' in her surname is soft as a whisper and the 't' is silent. This must be quite a bore, but she's actually quite likeable when you get to know her.

"My dear Annalise, I have come to wish you well on your opening night. I'm sure you must be a bag of nerves. I was the same on my first night," she says.

Her blonde hair is a similar colour to mama's, perhaps a shade lighter from the lemon juice she uses to enhance what she told me she thinks of as her trademark. Seven years older, Elizabeth is "an old hand at the game," Mr Bamford said. Her talent is apparently legendary in London circles, and she is very familiar with Mr Francis who she calls "my darling Ronald."

I note he always looks elsewhere when she says this as though he is uncomfortable.

"Oh yes, you're right I'm very nervous, Elizabeth," I lie, but I'm not sure why, "thank you for coming to see me to wish me well."

"Not at all, not at all, we girls must stick together," she winks conspiratorially my way and I smile at my new friend.

"Here she is, the girl of the hour."

Papa strides into the room with mama on his heels. He's dashing in his dinner suit and bow tie and mama has a new navy-blue satin dress for the occasion. She looks sideways at Elizabeth, her disdainful expression telling me my friend's presence is not welcome. She's become quite the mother-figure and I think mama's nose has been put out of joint.

Dear mama, there's only one person who could ever fill the motherly void in my heart, please don't worry, I'd like to tell her. But I don't want to mention it.

Elizabeth bids us farewell and heads off to join the gathering audience.

"You see, Garrison," mama says, "that dress makes her appear far too grown up for her tender years. I told you."

Smiling between his us papa says, "Yes, but remember Annelise is giving a performance tonight and playing the part of a woman and not a young girl."

Mama flops in a chair and looks as though she can't be bothered continuing the argument. She blows out loudly but then smiles at papa. He smiles back before he turns to me.

"I have a surprise for you," he says.

Mr Greenacre puts his head around the door as though he's been waiting for his cue. I gasp and clap my hands. Mrs Greenacre has been unwell and I thought he wouldn't be able to attend my opening night. Oh, joy of joys, I'm so happy to see him.

"Come, Clara, let us both leave them to it a moment and take our seats on the front row. Annalise, this is the night your future finally begins."

I close my eyes as he kisses my forehead, feeling like a small child.

Folding my arms around mama I whisper, "If it wasn't for you, mama I would not be here tonight. I will never forget the sacrifices you've made for me, thank you."

She pulls away to look deeply into my eyes and it's as though we're the only two people in the room.

"Any mother would do the same, my darling," she says, blowing me a kiss on her way out.

"You have been very lucky to have such supportive parents," Mr Greenacre says.

His new haircut makes him look different, younger, and he has on what I think is a brand-new dinner suit. He's made such an effort for me.

"You were never destined for ordinariness, my dear yet for one so young to be honoured with your own gala evening is remarkable."

Blushing, I look at the floor and think quickly what to say to cover my embarrassment.

"I hope you don't jinx the evening now, Mr Greenacre, not after all your efforts to get me here."

I'm glad when we laugh together, and my awkwardness at his praise disappears.

"All you must do is stay calm this evening. But above all, you must believe in yourself and your capabilities."

Kissing his warm cheek, I smell only soap.

"Ready?"

I take his outstretched hand and we head to wait backstage for my big moment.

Mr Bamford is there already and shakes hands with Mr Greenacre. I watch how comfortable the two friends are with each other. They studied music together for many years and now they've decided to make me their shared focus.

A voice booms from the stage taking us unawares. The shuffling and coughing amongst the audience die down to a hush as I raise my eyebrows at my two mentors. They both grin and I walk to stand just behind the red velvet curtains. They almost match the colour of my dress.

"My lords, ladies and gentlemen, this evening the Royal Opera House, Covent Garden is pleased to introduce a young lady who we feel you will take to your hearts; a new star who will light up the firmament of our humble stage for many years to come. Please give a warm welcome for her very first performance at the Royal Opera House to—there is a short pause for effect—Miss Annalise Patterson."

This is my cue. As I step from behind the barrier of the curtain, I had imagined it would feel surreal, but this is not the case. I feel very much a part of my surroundings. On the front row mama and papa join the clapping of the audience as the orchestra strikes the first chords of *Casta Diva*. I await my cue from Mr Francis.

Now finally my voice begins to reverberate around the auditorium as my body tells the story of the beautiful piece depicting the calm before a storm. I am floating within the words, the fluidity of movement of my hands and arms, nothing else matters at this moment. This stage is my new home, and the audience almost does not exist. My calling has finally been answered.

But too soon the moment is lost as the aria comes to an end and the music floats away to silence. My throat is tightly knotted so moved am I by the thick atmosphere surrounding me.

When the applause begins it is hesitant, almost uncertain and I look to mama and papa for encouragement. I need look no further. Mama is dabbing her eyes whilst papa's face is flushed and beaming my way.

The sound of clapping becomes more powerful until the noise fills every nook and cranny of the vast space and I fall into it. My eyes scan the sea of faces, all are smiling, some turn to their neighbour and exchange words; there are shouts of brava everywhere but before these can build Mr Seidl is tapping his baton and readying the orchestra for my next piece—Inneggiamo. This moment is a thing of dreams.

By the time I finish last piece of the evening I can see only one face and no others. It is the face of a smartly dressed dark-haired man in the box above me to my right.

As the crowd climb to their feet to continue their applause, the man inclines his head in my direction. I don't understand how I can possibly know, but this man is trying to tell me something.

Something I cannot hear yet, but I'm certain in the not-too-distant future I shall.

Chapter 12

1892—Lilian

Throwing another log on the fire, Stevie replaces the iron pan on the range. He checks the clock, but it's stuck at eleven minutes past two as being far from a creature of habit, Lilian hasn't wound it. Darkness is descending on the room and there's no sign of her. He shakes his head. This food will not be fit for man, woman nor beast if she's not back soon, he thinks.

A 'Molly Washup,' that's what Samuel would call him for doing chores, but the girl must eat, and her mother and sister are at their wits end. He should be cruel to be kind but perhaps it's more a case of can he be.

Is this the real Lilian or was she the young girl he knew long ago? So much has changed since that day in the ginnel, but that young girl is no more.

He's been sent with a message, and he chews his thumb nail as he stirs the pan absentmindedly.

Blowing out his cheeks when he hears the gate his relief quickly swings to apprehension. The next hour does not bode well for them. He peers from behind the greying nets to see her walking up the path. What a sight to behold she is, swinging a lantern from her hand, a culled rabbit draped around her neck. If he wasn't so pensive, he would laugh.

"So, the wanderer returns," he says, taking the stew from the range.

Dropping the rabbit unceremoniously on the table Lilian plonks herself down on the kitchen chair to take off her muddied boots. Her face is streaked with filth, her short nails darkened by the reddish-brown concoction of blood and dirt.

"I could say the same to you," she says, padding in her stockinged feet towards the sink. She lathers the soap and washes her hands and face, a tide mark hanging around her neck still, before drying herself with a ragged piece of sacking.

Even with her hair falling from its braid to hang around her ears she is still a beautiful woman if only she knew it ... or cared.

"I've had a lot to sort out since dada died, Lily, but this place is a bloody shambles.

"You sound like an old washer woman, Stevie, it's not that bad. Anyway, I've more important things to think about than dusting."

He wants to say, "Like what, Lily, what are all these important things you need to attend to?" but he doesn't. Instead, he heaps stew into two bowls he washed up himself and cuts the bread he brought from the bakery into thick doorstops.

He hands her a bowl as she rests her feet on the hearth rail to warm. Taking a seat in the opposite chair he dips his bread into the stew to enjoy a bite of it.

"Thanks," she says, "I'm sorry about your dada. I feel bad I didn't go to the funeral, but I didn't want to risk running into mam and our Sissy."

Stevie sets his bread down in his bowl and stares at his friend so long she begins to shift in her seat.

"What's up with you?" Lilian asks, her mouth swollen with food.

"Look, it's no good us skirting around the issue any longer—we're all worried about you. I know you like your independence and I for one admire you for it, but you're becoming more eccentric by the day, if that's the word. I'm starting to wonder if you can even look after yourself anymore."

Lillian calmly takes a mouthful of food unprovoked by his attack on her character.

"I've managed so far, Stevie. I've told you before, the thought of living a life like our Sissy makes my stomach heave. I'd lose my mind, I tell you, all that conforming and bending to fit in with other people who are doing the same conforming and bending to fit in with more other people. They just need to work out it's a vicious circle because they're all as miserable as sin."

Staring at her profile bathed in firelight he has the bitter-sweet sensation he often gets around Lilian, somewhere between love and desperation.

"And are you happy, Lily?" Stevie asks, finally giving up on his stew.

She snorts, "I would be if mam and our Sissy would leave me be and accept me as I am. Do you hear me telling anybody what to do, how to live their lives?"

Looking around the room he closes his eyes briefly and sighs. To be fair to her she doesn't interfere in anyone else's life.

Lilian turns her head to look at him, taking in all his sparkling cleanliness as she thinks of it. He's always smartly dressed when out of his overalls, and she needs to look closely to see the grey in his red hair. She can't deny she's missed him not coming round these last couple of weeks. But she knows he's leading up to something. She's known almost since she walked into the house because she knows Stevie back to front and inside out, like he does her.

"Come on then, let's have it," she says, clattering the bowl on the hearth and pushing her hair behind her ears.

For once she's giving him her full attention so Stevie's wrong footed. He can't remember the last time she was so alert and focused on anything other than herself.

His breath leaves his mouth in a long gush of air. He wants to go home.

"Well, as you ask, it's Mr Whitworth. I think your mam has got in his ear and he's sent me with a message."

Lilian's brow knits. She hasn't heard his name in so long it comes as a side sweep and her entire body tenses to it. What message could Garrison Whitworth have for her? The arrangement they've had has run like clockwork up until this very moment, so she hasn't needed to think back to that time much.

Stevie stands up to walk to the window. He can't see anything other than shadows in the darkness, but he'd prefer not to look at Lilian when he tells her what he's come to say.

"Mr Whitworth … Mr Whitworth says if you don't go back to work in the canteen, he won't be paying your rent after this month."

Her mouth gapes. It's such a simple request to most, working in a canteen, but not to Lilian.

"Does mam know he pays my rent?" she asks.

If she does know this would shed a whole different light on the matter. How could she explain away why her former employer was paying her rent?

"No, of course not. He just can't think of any other way to get you back to work. You're upsetting your mother so much living like this, everybody on the street can see it, not just him. I can see it."

Lilian is the last person who would deliberately want to upset her mother, but she hated the routine of working like a toothache. She's not lazy, she just can't abide people and rules, and the other women hated her for it.

So, one day she stopped going to work in the canteen and nothing happened. How could anything possibly happen when Mr Whitworth owed her so much? She was free, a black cloud hanging over her floating away. She was happy.

And now she must wait for the cloud to return and follow her, all over again.

Stevie leaves the window to crouch at her knee.

"I know, you don't have to tell me how you feel about it, I even understand. But worrying about you is taking its toll on your mam. She loves you that's the only reason why she's bothered so much. No mother would want this kind of life for her daughter."

Lilian isn't listening anymore.

"How dare he?" she whispers, though the tone is menacing, "After all I've done for him, how dare he even consider putting me in this position?"

Stevie leans over to take her hand, but she bats him away, her face glowing with anger. The rejection wounds him, but he must stand firm because he knows he's the only one who has a chance of making her see sense.

"Look Lily, you can just try it for a month or two and then find something else if you hate it as much as before. You could do some cleaning, or I don't know, some farm work if you're so miserable. You don't have to stay at Whitworths."

Bowing her head, a tear falls on her skirt. Oh, Lily you're breaking my heart, he thinks. He tries one more time and this time she doesn't pull away when he takes her hand. Should he ask her again to marry him? He'd marry her tomorrow if she'd have him, purely for convenience and to give her some stability. But marriage would put her in a cage, so she'd grow to slowly but surely hate him. He could pay her rent, but she would think it inappropriate. Unconventional she may be, but Lilian is still a lady.

When she lifts her head, she stares into his eyes. He holds her gaze fast and doesn't look away because he can't. Waiting a long moment he nibbles his lower lip, unsure how to react to what she's revealing to him.

Instead of seeing a broken doll behind the tears, he sees a resolve that alarms him, unsettles him even.

After all these years he thought he knew her, but he's just this very day realised Lilian Reid is not a woman to be trifled with.

Chapter 13

1892—Clara

Clara is utterly bored. The more lavish these post-concert parties have become the less sparkle they have for her. At first, they were intimate and lively as everyone was able to interact in a small group and everyone could have their say. Now she's become invisible once more.

She would love to be tucked up in bed with her husband, even if it must be at the *Hotel Cecil*. Garrison now considers the suite there a home from home as Mr Bamford hoped, and home for Clara is where her husband lays his head.

Viscount Howarth is regaling everyone with the wonder of her daughter in a boorish voice to all who will listen. Boorish is perhaps an unfair description but he's not her favourite person though she knows she hides this fact well. The man is obsessed with her daughter, and Annalise is undoubtedly smitten. She has all the signs of a girl in love; that soft glow she often spots on her own face when she catches herself in the mirror. Oh, the Viscount has the looks and the charm and the money, but how can he possibly settle with a girl of Annalise's standing in society. She may be of independent means nowadays, but his father, the Earl of Shrewsbury will no doubt already have a bride in mind and it will be one with land and money. Clara is certain of it because isn't this how it works in aristocratic circles? Her daughter is set to have a rude awakening so she must find a way to protect her from it. She thinks of how in her own youth, she didn't listen to her own mother because she thought her attitudes outdated. She may well need to accept Annalise will be the same. Motherhood is such a minefield, Clara thinks, even when our children have grown.

Her eyes scroll across the droves of people milling around the dazzling ballroom. She doesn't need to look far to spot Annalise in her now trademark dress of the deepest scarlet. If she has one dress, she has thirty, all too similar in Clara's mind but even she had to admit the colour suits Annalise to a tee. She graciously conceded defeat on the issue months ago. At this moment, standing under the candelabra Analise is in the spotlight. Many an eye is upon her, but Clara is the one who catches Annalise's eye.

She watches on as her daughter almost glides across the room in her direction, turning the heads of men and women alike. Such an elegant young lady, but then she was even before her public persona; her mentors had no need to cultivate grace and elegance with her. In fact, they must have been laughing big apples because she stepped into this life as effortlessly as a duckling to water.

Nowadays Clara admits to growing fond of Mr Francis and Mr Bamford and she doesn't worry about Annalise being in safe hands any longer.

"Ah, here she is," Viscount Howarth says, "Annalise come join us."

His evening suit is cut of the latest style, his curly hair teased into neat black curls. They would have beautiful children, Clara thought suddenly before quickly reproaching herself.

Smiling, Annalise takes her mother's hand, and they greet the small group of women fanning themselves in the summer heat. The viscount is constantly surrounded by women which is another concern of Clara's.

The day is waning but sadly the heat is not, and the copious number of candles are only adding to the suffocating temperature. How she'd love to kick off her shoes under her dress as her feet will surely burst open the seams, they're so swollen.

"Mrs Whitworth, you must be so proud of your daughter. She is the toast of society and in no time at all," the viscount says as though addressing his audience, "Tell me, where did her stage name of Patterson come from?"

Clara smiles affectionately at her daughter, squeezing her hand. If one more person says how proud I must be of my daughter, I will scream she thinks. Of course, she's proud of her, it's a moot point, one not even worth mentioning any longer.

"Patterson was my mother-in-law's maiden name, Viscount Howarth, it was my husband's suggestion. We felt it had a fine ring to it and complemented the name of Annalise well," Clara says quietly.

She doesn't mention how Garrison suggested her own maiden name first. She neatly sidestepped the matter insisting Patterson was a far better match with Annalise.

How Clara wishes she didn't mind being the centre of attention. She should be growing used to it, having been pushed into the limelight more often of late. She's relieved when Garrison arrives by her side and warmly greets the viscount. They have become friendly over the months, and she worries the viscount has Garrison in the palm of his hand. She must talk to him about it though their time together is limited lately. Late nights, early starts, days apart all mean they are losing connection to her mind, and this worries her more than anything.

Clara feels the drop of Annalise's hand as she moves further into the circle. If she's not careful her heart will be broken by the viscount Clara thinks, and the first break is the most profound, the most devastating. She's suddenly overcome less by the heat and more by the situation.

Waiting for a lull in Garrison's conversation, Clara asks if they might leave as the summer heat is making her lightheaded. She's fighting the urge to flee the ballroom in a dramatic fashion most unlike her.

Her husband's face contorts with concern, "Of course, my love," he says making his excuses to the viscount.

Garrison speaks to Annalise, and she appears almost immediately by her mother's side once more. They follow the viscount to the foyer of the ballroom and listen to him relaying the instructions to a footman for his carriage to be brought to the front entrance at once. Clara can't abide a fuss, but she's glad of the escape and the night air, warm or otherwise. The family thank the viscount for his kindness as they're helped one by one into the carriage.

"Not at all madam. I hope you feel better in the morning after a good night's sleep. Mr Whitworth, Miss Patterson," he says inclining his head in turn through the carriage window.

The carriage disappears into the darkening streets and the clattering of horses' hooves on the cobbles signal the growing distance between them and Clara can finally breathe.

"I'm sorry to you both for bringing the evening to a sudden end," she says, looking between her husband and daughter.

They open their mouths to allay her concerns, but she raises her hand.

"It's become so irregular nowadays for us to be together without other people present. I simply must speak to you whilst I have my nerve."

"What is it, mama?" Annalise asks, her treacly eyes wide with concern.

Garrison is watching Clara intently as her hand flutters to her throat flushed with nerves.

"Annalise, I've observed that you've developed deep feelings for the viscount over many months. I hope you won't try to deny it. But Garrison, I also feel you are encouraging this liaison. This is a dangerous position for you to be in Annalise. As talented and celebrated as you are in London society nowadays, we must understand our station and his. I think the viscount will be expected to marry a person of the Earl and Countess Shrewsbury's standing and choosing."

Fanning herself manically now Clara slumps in her seat relieved of a terrible burden. She realises this is the first time she's breathed normally in weeks, perhaps months.

Garrison grasps his wife's hand and raises it to his lips.

"Clara, do you really think I would make a decision about our daughter's future without consulting you first and Annalise for that matter? I learnt my lesson that night with Mr Greenacre but even then, no decision had been made. I enjoy the company of Viscount Howarth and I know he is Annalise's greatest fan. We have plenty to thank him for as a patron. However, any involvement of a romantic nature with her is another matter entirely."

Annalise watches her parents together in their own world a moment or two before staring out of the carriage window. The streets of London are aglow with candlelight and blackness in equal measure, and she has seen so little of it. She misses Yorkshire and Hardcastle sometimes, but she doesn't want to seem ungrateful for their sacrifices. Once she was never away and now, she's hardly ever there. As with everything in life a balance would be preferable.

"Annalise?" her mother says.

Turning to look at her parents Annalise wafts her own fan in front of her face, overcome with emotion.

"Mama, papa, please," she says, her voice cracking, "you're quite right mama, I have indeed fallen in love; completely and utterly head over heels in love."

She watches as her parent's glance at each other and then back in her direction, the same incredulous look on their faces.

"But you don't need to concern yourself about Viscount Howarth and his intentions, mama. Whether or not I am the girl for him I have no idea ... but he is most certainly not the man for me."

Chapter 14

1892—Sissy

Thank heavens it's summer, Sissy thinks. She's unable to stomach the idea of going inside that midden of a cottage her sister lives in. If it wasn't for her mother, she wouldn't be here at all.

"You can't have the penny and the bun, Lilian. You've been living off the kindness of strangers for too long and it's time to live in the real world like the rest of us."

Sissy sniffs in a self-righteous manner, annoying Lillian. This is generally how she feels in her sister's presence.

"Oh, give it a rest, Sissy, will you? Garrison Whitworth is hardly a stranger, and neither is Stevie. I get what I need from the land mainly and if Stevie wants to bring the odd bit of wood or a loaf of bread then I'm not going to throw his kindness back in his face."

The sisters are sitting on the makeshift bench in the back yard of Lilian's cottage, perching as far apart as they can manage as though denying their relationship. Sissy looks side on at Lilian and sees her dress has been patched twice at the front and she noticed another three patches when she was sitting down to shell peas on her lap. What a fright she is to Sissy's mind; she's ashamed of her.

Sissy thinks back to when they used to shell peas around their mother's cosy kitchen table at least twice a week. They'd gossip and chat about the mundane, no idea of the unrest to come.

We won't be shelling peas together today that's for sure, Sissy thinks. If I wasn't so furious, I could cry. Lilian landed on her feet living at the cottage rent free right enough. Now, if it had been my cottage, I would have kept it like a little palace. Jack and Harry would have loved the freedom of the farm and the fields beyond. What a different childhood my boys would have had. Such gifts are wasted on this ragamuffin.

"Well, mam wants to know if you're going back to the canteen. If not, she's washing her hands of you, and I'm inclined to do the same. You've had a free ride for long enough."

Lilian tuts then puffs out her cheeks.

"Oh, how bitter you are, Sissy, I'd hardly call it a free ride. I've had a price to pay. You couldn't get your own way and now you blame me. You could have left Samuel and got a little job and a little house but no, you wanted to live on Bright Eye Lane. Nowhere else was good enough. Can you imagine what it would have been like with us living together? I think you might find we had a lucky escape."

Sissy's face is puce.

"If you were anywhere near normal, it would have been fine but you're like a wild animal. What Stevie sees in you I have not a clue. What happened to you, Lilian? Me and mam have talked about it until we're blue in the face, but we can't see what happened to change you so much."

Lilian casts the bowl aside quickly, so the peas are strewn on the vegetable patch. She jumps up and glowers at her sister.

"I can understand mam being in the dark, but you, Sissy. The baby happened, that's what. The baby happened and you bloody well know it."

When Sissy gets to her feet, she towers over Lilian saying, "The baby, the baby, that's all I ever hear, and the excuse has worn thin. I'm sick of it, do you hear me, sick to my bloody back teeth."

Sissy raises her hand just as Stevie walks out of the back door. He was waiting inside to give them some privacy but kept a watchful eye on proceedings.

Throwing himself between the two sisters he says, "No you don't, Sissy, there's no need for that."

Sissy's chin is wet with spittle, and she wipes it with the back of her hand. Has she become as bad as her sister, like a crazed animal herself? Dropping back down on the bench she looks down at the ground, shame making her dizzy. She looks up at Stevie with his protective arm around Lilian as though she's a child; she thinks of her as an errant child sometimes. *Why couldn't I have married someone like Stevie instead of my cold calculating husband?* She knows the answer well enough: Samuel earned better money at the pit, and she thought she would have status in the village. The price has been heavy.

"Just do us all a favour and marry him, why won't you?" Sissy says, all the fight flowing from her boots and into the soil. She's tired of it all.

"Now that's none of your business," Stevie says brusquely.

Lilian steps from his protective embrace telling Stevie she's quite capable of speaking for herself.

"Look, Sissy, I love Stevie, I might not tell him, but I do. Even though I don't tell him, he knows it because he understands me better than anyone else, even you and mam. He's well aware marriage isn't for me. I've seen what marriage did to you for one thing and I'm not taking a chance."

"Marriage didn't do anything to me, only Samuel did," Sissy says, running a hand down her face, "Stevie is a gentleman, and you'd do well to snatch his hand off while you've got the chance. I can't see him hanging around forever, waiting for you to change your mind."

Lilian glances at Stevie who's staring impassively down the yard towards the farmhouse in the distance. Will he wait forever she wonders, does he want a home, a family? She knows in her heart that he does, he's always wanted one. I'm depriving him of it all is her sad conclusion.

"You've got until tomorrow to decide whether you're going back to work or not," Stevie tells Lilian without looking her way, "That's when the rent's due by my calculation."

Sissy walks to the little gate and waits before she opens it.

"What are you going to do?" she asks her sister.

The sunshine on Lilian's face highlights the grubbiness of her complexion. When was the last time she had a proper bath, Sissy wonders.

Stevie finally turns his head to look at Lilian, desperate to know the answer to the question himself.

Pulling the bucket up from the well, Lilian swigs a handful of the freezing water as the others wait to see if they will get a response.

"The way I see it," Lilian says, "is that the oh so high and mighty Garrison Whitworth is in no position to be calling the shots with me."

Chapter 15

1896—Annalise

"Dear me, another performance. Howie. As grateful as I am, I must rest my voice on occasion if you don't mind."

Viscount Howarth may be "his lordship in high society but to me he's now plain old Howie, at least in our private world. Laughing he takes a large bite of his scone, brushing his palms together to be rid of the crumbs. How improper he can behave in my company nowadays. I can't help but smile to myself.

"Make hay while the sun shines, my sweet. Yes, you are in demand—enjoy it and reap the rewards while you can until you have a brood of children strapped to your bosom," he says.

How I look forward to his company. Mr Bamford and Mr Francis are a little put out, but I still have two regular performances each Saturday afternoon and evening at the opera house.

"You know, I would like to see my husband sometimes. He's a patient man but I like to spoil him when I can."

"Oh, piffle. Anybody would think you're a wide-eyed newlywed to hear you speak."

"Not quite that after eighteen months, but I miss him it's true. Is that so wrong of me?"

Running his fingers through his curls he gets up from the table to sit by the fire and light a cigar. I wait as he's deep in thought, smoke rings dancing around his head before drifting aimlessly toward the ceiling.

"You know I'm only jealous. One day I hope to find the love you have found with Hugo," he says.

His voice is laced with a touch of melancholy. He tells me often he's surrounded by people but I'm the only person who really matters, who truly knows him. He can never be sure if others are after his title and money, but for the time being at least, he's managing to avoid a marriage of convenience. His mother twitters about his lack of commitment often but he uses humour to deflect her. He's expecting to be summoned to his father's study any moment to discuss his future. The thought of it makes him queasy and he knows that eventually he will be forced to comply. He can't risk being cut off in favour of his younger brother.

"What did Hugo have that I didn't? Howie says, half-heartedly. He knows the answer to his pleading many times, that he could offer me the lap of luxury with a title, no less.

"Ah, the all-important question, Howie, for which there is no easy answer. You have it all you really do, and you mustn't think otherwise. Let your barriers down a little and see what happens. If you can do it with me, you can surely do it with others."

Dying out his cigar he stretches out his long legs saying, "But you forget, Annalise my dear, you are a very special, in fact extraordinary lady. Your voice alone however exceptional, would not be enough to make you the toast of London."

My mind wanders to Hugo. I know I'm his special lady now though I wouldn't believe it at first when we met at the opera house. He presented himself as the Honourable Hugo Harper, like Howie, a patron of the Royal Opera House and, he declared, my most ardent fan.

"Miss Patterson, I've been simply dying to meet you," he said when we were introduced in my dressing room.

Mama had returned to the hotel and Mr Bamford was a busy man so made the decision I could be left alone unchaperoned.

When he touched his lips to my hand, I had a brand-new sensation which has now become familiar. It was rooted deep in my stomach, and it lingers still. The viscount is dashing and fascinating company, but Hugo speaks quietly to my soul, sometimes even without uttering a single word.

He hung onto my every word that day and then found what I thought were quite feeble reasons to seek out my company twice more. To be honest, I didn't mind and admit to engaging in a little cunning myself so we could be alone.

It was on the second occasion when he informed me that he had an ulterior motive.

"You have heard the name Arthur Rayburn," he teased.

"Who hasn't," I replied, wondering why he should wish to discuss the esteemed Arthur Rayburn of *The Times,* whose reviews could make or break any theatrical or operatic production.

He paused, searching for the right words: "In your presence I find myself unable to maintain a deceit that has served me well for several years."

"A deceit Mr Harper," I challenged, a frown stealing across my face as I began to contemplate the folly of meeting him alone.

Realising my discomfort, he took my hand.

"Please, I apologise, it's not as you might think."

His hand was warm not hot, giving me a pleasant sensation of comfort.

"I am Arthur Rayburn," he declared, a little too proudly perhaps.

"You are not sir; you are the Honourable Hugo Harper. As you have presented yourself to me," I say, full of indignation, "and to others I add. Howie, erm Lord Shrewsbury says he knows your parents."

Hugo, or was it Arthur, raised a half-smile, his head bowed slightly. "It seems my little subterfuge has been more successful than I thought. Arthur Rayburn is a nom de plume, I created Arthur to disguise my real identity."

"But why, pray – you have a good name and reputation," I replied.

"Precisely. It was to save my parents' blushes and I suppose I thought it would make me appear more a man of the people.

I laughed when he told me this eventually, admiring his honesty.

Hugo explained how writing had always been his passion and all he ever wanted to do; but it was hardly becoming for someone of his standing to take paid employment. However, he had confided in his parents and although it was frowned upon, he won them over by agreeing to write under a pseudonym, ensuring a discrete distance between Hugo and his alter ego, Arthur. I came to suspect that some people in the business, like Mr Francis, knew his secret, but were happy to maintain the pretence.

Hugo was as interested as he was interesting. By the end of our third meeting, I knew we were falling in love. I wouldn't accept we had fallen in love at first sight as this seemed preposterous then. Now though I wonder if we did as mama said she and papa fell in love at first sight.

We moved into Sutton Manor, one of his father's properties in Yorkshire, a most generous wedding gift. I had confided to Hugo that I wanted to be closer to mama, even if it meant more travelling to and from London.

I think of our wedding night, the memory often keeping me warm when we're hundreds of miles apart. I endured a very awkward conversation with mama in the run up to the wedding, glad when it was over. But in the end, I felt so far removed from how I expected to feel: afraid and hesitant to give myself to my new husband.

Taking off my nightgown, Hugo let it slip to the floor, so the white cotton rippled at my feet. I was unabashed, enjoying the headiness of the pleasure written all over his face. Even before that moment I have always felt him to be part of me. The pulsation between my legs was new and wonderfully wicked. He pushed my hand to his groin and pressed it firmly, so he sprang to life. Our breath was hot on each other's faces as his hands roamed my breasts, tweaking my nipples to make me moan. Though I had limited expectation nothing scared me, everything came naturally, even his fingers inside me first before then slipping himself inside me. Both of us couldn't help ourselves crying out with the wanton passion flowing through our bodies. This is love, I thought, this is pure lustful love between a man and a woman.

Now he teases me, telling me I've emasculated him as I'm the breadwinner in our house. But there's no sign of emasculation with Hugo and he lives happily in his world of writing most of the time though I know he misses me. Never needing to work, he devotes himself to his novel, an epic tale of a humble soldier's life during the Napoleonic Wars, supplemented with his theatre reviews and essays for The Times. Hugo loves to write from the point of view of the ordinary person whom he considers to be the real hero of the story. I often think he is a man out of time and place.

Howie's voice startles my mind back into the room.

"How did you know with Hugo," he asks me, "What signs should I be on the lookout for?"

He's looking at me intently and I almost wonder if he's reading my mind. Blushing I pat down my hair primly trying to block out the recollections of Hugo for the sake of propriety. One should not be having such thoughts in the presence of a viscount.

I look up at the painting of Hugo I had commissioned, and which hangs pride of place on the wall of my suite at the *Cecil*. His fair hair flops in a cowlick to stop just above his eyebrows no matter how hard he tries to tame it to do otherwise. I find it so becoming though it drives him to distraction.

A small smile tilts my lips as I stare at the painting underneath the candlelight.

"In the end you won't need to look for the signs, Howie. They are waiting patiently to reveal themselves at exactly the right time … and not a moment before."

Chapter 16

1896—Lilian

So, the day has finally dawned Lilian thinks, pinning her wet hair into a swirl at the nape of her neck. She found a blue cotton dress from years ago in the back of the wardrobe and she's washed and pressed it into shape. Her nails are clipped, her cheeks pinched for colour and as she twirls in the reflection of the glass in the window, she barely recognises the person staring back at her. She can't remember the last time she took note of her appearance, it's generally the last thing on her mind.

"How do you do," she says to herself with a small curtsey, "I think I scrub up well though I say it myself."

She's still shaken from Sissy's visit yesterday and she narrowly missed a clobbering as Stevie called it—she was lucky he came out when he did. We know how to bring out the worst in each other, that's for certain, she thinks but then isn't that all sisters, siblings even. There was a time when Sissy was the person Lilian turned to first in times of trouble, especially after their father died. They were tight but mainly because their mother had enough to worry about with being widowed so young. They rarely argued then, as they both would have hated to add to her burden.

The day is warm, so she doesn't need a shawl as she steps out for the long walk ahead. She knows a short cut over a stile and takes note of all she can forage on the return journey, annoyed with herself she didn't bring a basket. Her damp neck tickled by the summer breeze she's as glad as ever to be outdoors.

When she wonders if she should call in at her mother's, her mood is changed. She's only over the road from the factory so there's no excuse, except Lilian avoids seeing her mother just as much as she avoids seeing her sister. She has plenty to say about her disappointment in her daughter's choice of lifestyle yet how can someone be something they're not? The façade will drop sooner or later, and how she tried to conform for her mother alone for long enough seems to count for nothing.

Bright Eye Lane looms ahead, the imposing chimney stack of Whitworth's displaying the company name vertically in brass lettering. It's an impressive landmark but it does nothing to impress Lilian as she meanders down the street, dodging the sparkling white sheets hanging to dry. She knows she'll have to call in at her mother's as she'll be spotted by somebody, and she wouldn't want to hurt her feelings.

Pushing one of the double doors of the entrance to Whitworths she steps into the stone flagged foyer. An internal window shows the carpenters workstations neatly lined with tools ready for the morning. Stevie will have left, she timed it perfectly, but she knows he will have thought of nothing else but her all day. His office door is ajar, so she peers around to see his desk and chair remembering how proud she was of him when he was made foreman. Garrison Whitworth leans on him more nowadays especially as he's out of town regularly.

Up the stairs she goes in search of Garrison, strangely without any sense of trepidation. He's been a distant figure since Annalise was born but he kept his word and looked after her up until now.

She spots the gilt framed newspaper cuttings of Annalise lining the corridor. How delighted Garrison will at the beautiful, talented lady she has become. Stevie sometimes likes to update Lilian about her glorious rise to fame.

She stares now at a cutting from *The Times* newspaper from only last autumn and in the engraved image, sees nothing but a stranger. Her own flesh and blood, yet her heart is dull.

Stevie went to her wedding in York the year before and brought some cake back for her. Lilian now feels the same looking at the photograph as she did when she looked at the cake: removed, indifferent. Should she feel like this she wondered, had she grown hard and cold, or would anybody feel the same?

A distant clattering alerts Lilian to the fact Mrs Wagstaff is somewhere in the building. She'd rather she didn't run into her so moving away from the photograph Lilian knocks on Garrison Whitworth's office door.

After a delay of a few seconds, she tries again, knocking a little louder. Silence is the only response. Checking right then left down the long corridor she tries the handle and when the door moves slightly ajar, she drops her hand. This is his private space, and she shouldn't even be contemplating entering here unless invited, she knows this. But she must be certain he has left because if so, she must return tomorrow and she'd rather not. Anxiously, Lilian heaves her shoulders and strides into the office as though walking into the lion's den.

Her foot over the threshold she takes a moment to check she's alone before she digests the grandness of the room. It has the right balance with the masculine desk and bookcase then the softness of the well-worn leather chairs flanking the cosy fireplace. She imagines Stevie and Garrison Whitworth chatting by the fire that day she asked for Stevie's help and swallows down the memory. Her hands hang helplessly by her side.

What to do now she wonders.

Well, apparently there's nothing else for it she thinks, I must leave and pay a visit to my mother as planned. Tomorrow she will return earlier because the rent on the cottage will be overdue. Her lips purse at the brass neck of the big man. Laying down the law and delivering ultimatums does not sit well with Lilian … and especially under the circumstances.

Heading to the window she stands behind the net curtain and sees her childhood home opposite. Mr Whitworth has had a prime viewing spot of her house for many a year it seems. Lilian feels homesick for the simple times she spent in those four walls, before her father died, when she wasn't a constant disappointment to her mother and sister. How they used to eat tea and shell peas around the table polished to a shine with beeswax by her mother every Tuesday morning without fail. Always a creature of habit and routine, she's sure her mother will still be sticking to the same old regime.

Oh, what's this she wonders. She can't move her legs though her stomach is flipping.

The door opens suddenly, and Mrs Wagstaff looks at Lilian with alarm then disdain, the cleaner's nose lifting and the corners of her mouth drooping as though she's discovered a bad smell. Her salt and pepper coloured hair is coming loose from her bun, and Lilian can see the two wiry hairs on her chin even from where she's standing. The cleaner stands with a bucket in her hand and for a moment Lilian thinks this might be a glimpse of her future self if she's not careful.

"What are you doing in here, miss, you've no right to let yourself in? I'll be telling Mr Whitworth in the morning," Mrs Wagstaff says.

Lilian raises to her full height, lifting her chin as she heads towards the door. Mrs Wagstaff steps to one side, watching her closely as though Lilian might snaffle something in her pocket on the way out.

"Please do, Mrs Wagstaff, please do. I will be returning tomorrow, and Mr Whitworth will be keen to see me, I'm sure," she says in a hoity toity tone.

As she closes the door behind her, Lilian isn't thinking of Mrs Wagstaff and her disdain any longer, her mind is elsewhere, preoccupied with the scene she has just witnessed from the window.

Across the lane, her mother was lighting the lamp with a taper; then turning as a man appeared in the room to put his arms around her waist and nuzzle his face into her hair.

The man was none other than Garrison Whitworth.

The cosy little scene is making her feel quite sick. Rushing back down the stone steps she bangs back the entrance door taking great gulps of warm summer air. She forgets for a moment that any resident of Bright Eye Lane might see her: her mind is full of images she can't unsee. This can't be possible surely, she thinks.

Dashing around to the rear yard of Whitworth's she leans her forehead against the cold brick wall and weeps. The shock is making her shiver uncontrollably. Eventually she wipes her face with the bottom of her dress to try and compose herself.

Engulfed by a sudden sense of loneliness and disappointment, Lilian sighs and slumps to the ground, hands grasped tightly around her shins. Soon she knows she must leave the temporary sanctuary of the yard.

But for so many reasons, it seems now is not the time to call in to see her mother after all.

Chapter 17

1897—Annalise

Train journeys are dull nowadays without mama's companionship. She may not have much interest in music per se, but I find it a refreshing change because music is generally the topic of conversation wherever I go.

Today, more than ever, I wish she were sitting by my side discussing some domestic issue or other minor distraction. Having received a telegram telling me I must return home "as a matter of urgency," the sum total of the information I have been given, my mind is tumbling over what could be the cause of such a vague and upsetting summons. My nerves are such that I don't know what to do with myself and almost ask the waiter for a brandy, but as ever my sense of politeness prevails.

I've never been called home before for any reason. For future reference I must ask papa to kindly remember that knowing nothing at all is far, far worse than knowing the full facts.

Has mama taken ill I wonder. They were both in fine fettle yesterday when I left, and mama was even planning a little soiree for Hugo and me next week. She wanted it to be just the four of us for a change.

As we pull into the train station at the side of Sutton Manor, I'm never more thankful for the luxury. Donald leans out of the driver's cab and waves as I alight. I lift my hand and raise a smile though I'm wondering where Sutcliffe has got to, hoping he might emerge still from the steam to help me. His absence only increases my apprehension; Sutcliffe has never been late to collect my bags and escort me home, not once.

"Can I help you with your luggage, madam?" the new conductor asks me.

I gesture to the shelter saying, "I would be grateful if you could leave my luggage in here, I'm sure my butler will be along any moment."

He does as I ask, and I press a shilling in his hand for his trouble.

"Thank you, madam," he says, shyly, "I confess I've been looking forward to meeting your ladyship."

Inclining my head, I thank him though by the time the train has left the station I've already set off through the gateway and into the grounds. The sound of the engine fades as the whistle blows a fond farewell. The afternoon is chilly, but the familiar smell of smoke coming from the chimneys is absent for once as I head up the path.

When I step into the hallway the atmosphere of the house is unsettling, cold and unwelcoming in every way. Where is everyone? Surely, they should be waiting for me when I've been summoned so urgently.

Mrs Littlewood appears at the cellar head, and we startle each other, her expression no doubt mirroring my own.

"Oh, madam, I'm so sorry, Mr Sutcliffe is with the master. We didn't know when to expect you."

"That's quite alright, Mrs Littlewood," I console her, "Please can you tell me where I can find Mr Hugo and Mr Sutcliffe."

Her eyes roll to her left in the direction of the staircase, but she doesn't speak. Her face is ghastly pale, her mouth set in a line.

"Are they in Mr Hugo's drawing room?" I ask.

She only nods and I fight the urge to shake her by the elbows before lifting my skirts high to bound up the stairs. After five hours of travelling and being kept in the dark I'm suddenly frantic with worry.

Before I reach the drawing room I am brought to a halt when I see Dr Lloyd leaving our bedroom. If it's not me in that room, it can only be one other person I deduce. This is too much; Hugo being unwell was not on my list of concerns.

"Miss Whitworth ... erm, Mrs Harper, I know you will be keen to see your husband, but before you do, I must speak with you downstairs."

Dr Lloyd is clearly unaware I am completely in the dark about the situation I realise. Holding tightly to the banister to steady myself I now curse my politeness under my breath; I'd like to shove him out of the way and run into the bedroom.

Instead, I obediently turn on my heels and retrace my steps down the stairs saying over my shoulder, "Certainly doctor, however I would be glad if you could be as succinct as possible to avoid further delay."

Minnie hurries from the parlour, coal bucket in hand just before we enter the room. I nod to Hugo's chair by the fire and Dr Lloyd perches on the edge of the seat running his tongue around his lips as though to unglue them. I find myself unable to sit down.

"Well, Mrs Harper," he says, "I'm afraid you must prepare yourself for a shock. Your … your husband is quite ill. He has a palsy, and these are never pleasant. As time is of the essence, I have no choice but to be frank and tell you the next twenty-four hours are critical."

I sit down heavily on the chaise opposite the fireplace. The drawn expression of our family doctor is highlighted by the watery sunshine of this February day. It alarms me. My family have barely needed to see him, and I suddenly realise how fortunate we were to be in such a position. Now, my luck has run out and my time has come to stand up and face the music.

"A palsy?" I ask quietly.

I'm hoping the doctor has a course of treatment in mind, so all can be well again.

But Dr Lloyd doesn't look like a man set to deliver encouraging news. I briefly wonder whether I should be seeking the advice of one of the leading physicians in Harley Street. I am acquainted with several through the theatre.

"Your butler found him collapsed early this morning. He was quick to raise the alarm but I'm afraid your husband is not himself and we have no way of knowing to what extent or for how long. All we can do is wait. In the meantime, you must brace yourself before you see him, my dear."

I sit staring at the doctor for a moment then closing my eyes briefly I heave a sigh. Enough is enough I decide and jump to my feet. I can't sit here any longer, I simply must go to Hugo. The compulsion to see him has become almost like adrenaline coursing through my body, pushing me up the stairs.

Outside our bedroom door I hesitate with my hand on the handle but only for a second before pushing it open. I feel a change in atmosphere as I cross the threshold as I did when I entered the house; like passing from one world to another. Everything is shifting and I have nothing to hold onto because Hugo is my rock.

The gas mantles have been turned low in an effort to try and calm him and in the semi-gloom I can see he's lying on the bed, eyes closed. Please no, has he already passed I wonder as I rush to put my ear to his mouth. I can't be certain if he's breathing so relief washes over me when I see the slow rise and fall of his chest. Thank God, I still have him, I think pressing a hand to my mouth.

My eyes go to his face, but now I take a step back from his bedside with shock. His skin is so translucent that I can almost see every sinew, every vein of his cheeks. He is still, apart from a periodic shaking of his right hand.

I don't know what can have happened in one short day. He showed no sign of illness whatsoever only yesterday. I close my eyes tightly to be rid of the sight. My Hugo, my darling boy now looks a stranger.

Pulling the chair from my dressing table I sit by his bedside and hold his other hand. It is limp and cold. He's going, he's leaving me I know it.

Oh, Annalise this is no time for histrionics, if he's leaving you these cannot be his final moments, trapped with a flailing wife at his bedside. I must draw strength from somewhere before I'm too late. I think of Maxwell Greenacre and his calming presence, hoping to stop my dark thoughts careering from a cliff.

"My darling, I'm so glad to be home," I say, my head on his forearm, "I'm here to get you well again, my love, your Annalise has come home to look after you."

My voice sounds odd but the sentiment behind them makes me catch my breath as I wipe a tear. If Hugo can hear me, and surely, he can if he's still breathing, I must give him some hope to cling to.

I sit in the quiet room whispering words of comfort when I feel none. I speak of anything which comes into my head: our first meeting, our wedding day, only wanting him to hear my voice.

Eventually I hear Dr Lloyd informing Sutcliffe he will return in no more than two hours. Raising my head, I stare at Hugo as he lays motionless like a body on a mortuary slab. I reach to smooth his fringe from his forehead over and over lost in the repetition. I try to convince myself he's only taking a nap until finally, my breathing returns to normal.

I'm startled by a banging on the front door. As the sound continues, I can't comprehend why the caller isn't ringing the customary doorbell. The urgent noise seems so far away I wonder if I've fallen asleep and dreaming.

"May I help you?" I hear Sutcliffe say.

I shake my woolly head to be sure I'm in a state of consciousness.

An unfamiliar voice breaks the silence saying, "Yes you may, sir. My name is Lilian Reid, and I would like to speak to the lady of the house if she will spare me a moment of her time."

Chapter 18

1897—Clara

Oh, the simple pleasure of a cup of tea by the fire, Clara thinks as she picks up her embroidery. She decided on two white lovebirds nestling inside a cage shaped as a golden heart and she commends herself on the symbolic choice.

What to give a daughter who has the world in the palm of her hand for her impending anniversary? This will suit her perfectly.

Clara manages to still see plenty of Annalise without traipsing back and forth to London thank goodness. Clara is a homebird and settling back in her nest makes her especially content having been away from home so much over the years. It's been a strain. But a mother must do what a mother must do and supporting Annalise is the most important thing. Now she's married Hugo, Clara is free to stay home more with the satisfaction she did her duty.

Will Annalise ever be content with hearth and home she wonders. Perhaps the patter of tiny feet might change her mind though this seems to be longer in coming than Clara imagined. Never mind, she thinks, my daughter has plenty of time for domesticity and she seems more than happy with her life at present. Hugo is her biggest fan and couldn't be more supportive.

For all his qualities Garrison would have found it hard to be accommodating of a wife who was away half the week gadding about the capital unless of course, it was to support their daughter. Hugo is an unconventional man, but then he has an artistic mind. Garrison despairs of his lack of business acumen though they've grown very fond of one another especially after Hugo's father died. Clara gently reminds her husband that Hugo has no need for business acumen as Annalise has her advisers who have made them a fortune and not a small one at that. A personal train station indeed, who would have thought it, never mind built it.

Clara and Garrison have planned the perfect soiree for Annalise and Hugo on Sunday. Mr & Mrs Greenacre will join them and there will be cake and singing around the piano. Her lips tilt softly, and a small sigh of contentment escapes her at the thought.

Life has settled beautifully to Clara's mind. Annalise is not only married but deeply in love which fulfils a mother's dearest wish. A loveless marriage would be a life sentence of misery.

A short rap on the door disturbs her tranquil moment and Cockcroft appears in the room.

"Madam, you have a visitor—a Miss Lilian Reid," he says, his expression displaying his confusion.

Clara's peaceful afternoon suddenly disappears into the distance and could not be further from her sights. Come Clara, she thinks, you must hold fast to your composure; you must not raise alarm bells with the staff.

"Ah yes, Cockcroft, I'm sorry it completely slipped my mind to tell you Miss Reid would be calling. Please show her in," she says returning her embroidery to the red velvet box by her chair. She notices her hands have suddenly developed a slight tremor.

As Cockcroft leaves, she jumps from her seat and quickly checks her hair in the mirror as she would for the arrival of any visitor. But she knows Lilian Reid is an extraordinary visitor and the sense of foreboding hangs low in the room.

Cockcroft reappears, ceremoniously announcing Miss Reid's arrival.

Lilian appears from around the door. Her dark eyes are wide, but she doesn't look afraid or indeed anything at all; her face is devoid of expression. Her shabby dress is clean, and she looks presentable but so out of place in the grand room.

How strange that the arrival of a person could shatter one's peace, so one is left flapping around in the wilderness. Why has Lilian descended on her today after all these years Clara wonders. Something has happened, she senses it.

"Ah, Miss Reid how good of you to call," Clara says, "Cockcroft, please could you bring us refreshments."

Lilian fixes a wooden smile in place and looks between Clara and her butler saying, "No ... thank you, that's quite alright. I shan't be here for very long."

Clara feels somewhere between relieved and anxious, an odd sensation she's never experienced before.

Bowing, Cockcroft leaves the two women alone and Clara stares at the closed door. She's at a loss. How to interact, how to even begin the conversation with the mother of her daughter when she thinks of herself as nothing less. Lilian is an unwelcome imposter this afternoon, yet Lilian has the upper hand.

"Won't you sit down a moment," Clara says at last.

Lilian hesitates before sitting opposite Clara. She places her small bag which has seen better days on her knee and sits primly. Clara would love to know what if anything she keeps inside that tiny bag as the sagginess of the cloth betrays an emptiness. She holds herself like a lady. Clara knows Lilian's mother to be a lady, though not in the literal sense. Lilian's wrapping may be a little worn, but still her beauty shines. The same beauty as her daughter, Clara thinks with a sharp stab of envy. Everyone assumes Annalise takes after her father with her good looks, she knows they do. Until now this has never bothered her.

Clara knows little of this girl, or should she now call her woman, and this has served her well over the years.

"So, this is a surprise, Lilian," Clara says mildly though she feels anything but mild, "How may I help you?"

Lilian studies the hearth rug a moment then allows her eyes to wander to Clara briefly before lowering them again. She seems sheepish and Clara realises she too would rather not be here. Her envy turns to a twinge of compassion.

"I didn't want to bother you, Mrs Whitworth. I don't want to stir up any unpleasant memories for either of us, believe me but ... but your husband ... Mr Whitworth has left me with no option."

Clara is gripped by a wave of nausea. What has Garrison done? She'd like to run upstairs and hide under the covers much like the day the police battered down the door to arrest her father. She knew then nothing would ever be the same and she knows it now.

"To what are you referring, Lilian?"

Lilian looks beyond Clara through the French doors and briefly takes note of the grounds. What different lives they both lead, Lilian thinks, and all Garrison Whitworth had to do was stump up a few coppers a week to pay her rent. That was all he had to do.

"I'm here because Mr Whitworth has refused to pay my rent for some months and now, I find myself in a difficult situation. My landlord is less than sympathetic to my situation, and it can't go on any longer."

She stares directly into Clara's eyes, startling her with the intensity.

"And I'd rather not point out this situation should never have come about. I'm sure you agree."

This is the first Clara had heard of the 'situation' Lilian has twice referred to. Garrison had not been forthcoming with this crucial piece of information but then he knows she would have objected to him playing with fire. She wonders if Lilian is telling the truth.

"I see, and what reason would my husband have for stopping the payments?"

Lilian smiles knowingly, happy to discover Clara was in the dark. This gives her more leverage.

"He said I must return to work at the canteen, or he'll stop paying my rent."

Clara's brow furrows slightly as she wonders why Lilian would find this objectionable.

"Ah, this seems a reasonable request. Perhaps your mother and sister were worried about you alone at the cottage all day every day. This isn't a healthy lifestyle for a young woman."

Lilian narrows her eyes. A reasonable request indeed she thinks. Perhaps if I had no ties whatsoever to the man this would be a reasonable request, but I've given him the world on a plate, made his all dreams come true.

"I can't lie, I'm disappointed you don't see things from my point of view, Mrs Whitworth. I thought you would be far more understanding. My lifestyle is perfectly healthy and no business of yours."

Clara tilts her chin upwards, unappreciative of the sudden turn in the tone of the conversation.

"I hope you haven't come here expecting me to go against my husband's wishes, my dear. Mr Whitworth has his reasons I'm certain of it and as a loyal wife, I must support him."

Clara knows Lilian holds many cards, but she will not betray her husband; more importantly she will not have her arm twisted up her back by this girl. She has perhaps forgotten she signed an agreement many years ago.

"You must support him," Lilian scoffs, standing up to throw her bag on the chair, "I think it might come as a shock to know your husband is not quite so loyal and supportive."

Their eyes lock. How dare she, Clara thinks, the audacity of her descending on her and ruining this quiet afternoon when she was doing no harm to anybody. She will speak to Garrison, but she will not be pushed around in her own home. Where will it all end? Today Clara must show her mettle and she's surprised to discover that defending her family is coming very easily. Lilian thought her a timid little mouse like everyone else.

She clears her throat.

"Ah, if you're alluding to the fact my husband is … seeing your mother and has been for some years, you're playing catch-up I'm afraid, Miss Reid. Your mother will not be the first and she certainly will not be the last. If she thinks this is the case, she is in for a rude awakening. Perhaps you would do well to warn her."

Lilian's cheeks flare as quickly as the rest of her face loses all colour like she's been roundly slapped.

After ringing the bell, Clara asks Cockcroft if he will see her guest out.

"Thank you for calling today, Miss Reid, I wish you well in your next chapter, sincerely I do."

Lilian trails behind the unsuspecting butler in a trance almost as though he's cast a spell. Conventional life is beckoning her like the devil to the bowels of hell. That life will be nothing less to her though she cannot make a single soul understand.

Except Stevie.

Clara waits for the front door to close and Cockcroft's footsteps to fade on the cellar steps so she's quite certain she's alone.

Then Clara pulls her handkerchief from the pocket of her dress and pushes it to her mouth. It's not long before she spoils the crispness of the cotton with her hot, bitter tears.

Chapter 19

1897— Garrison

"More pudding?" Elspeth asks.

Garrison smiles her way, eyes sparkling. How can two simple, even mundane words sound so comely he wonders. Elspeth is everything a woman should be—warm, shapely and particularly in her case, earthy. She's certainly all-woman.

As ever he can't help but remind himself that so too is Clara. When he's with Clara he thinks often of Elspeth and the reverse is true. This is different for Garrison as he never thought of other women when he was with his wife. How he loves Clara and for so many reasons. She has been a devoted wife and mother and he still finds her incredibly attractive even now she's in her fifties. Clara only has to look at him a certain way to give him that tingling sensation down his spine he knows and loves so well.

He's given up asking himself why he still feels the need to look elsewhere. He doesn't know the answer but he knows he can't help it. For a while, the question drove him to distraction, and he still feels greedy and grasping. Yet somehow, that's not enough to make him stop.

As Elspeth heaps more custard onto his second helping of jam roly-poly, she glances up at him.

"You look like a little boy waiting impatiently at the table for his dinner. Put your eyes back in," she teases.

"My eyes are not on stalks waiting for pudding, my love, exceptional as your cooking is."

Elspeth's cheeks redden, telling him that his smooth talking will never work with her. They both know it will.

She watches him tucking into her food at her kitchen table and wonders what excuse he's given to Clara. Elspeth never asks and she never will because she likes the little world which they've created just for the two of them.

Tongues wag on Bright Eye Lane for less but there's a little ginnel at the side of her house so Garrison can quickly slip in and out from over the road via the back gate. Four steps and he's in the ginnel. Just four little steps. Elspeth see this as fate, something that allowed their love to flourish in secret.

She keeps the front door locked so if anyone should knock, he can slip out the back door unseen. She has it all worked out to put the plan into action should the need ever arise. Often, she finds herself rehearsing it in her mind.

Garrison confessed he'd been watching her going about her business for years, even before Frank died. The sheer audacity of the man was her first thought when she found out, but then she couldn't help but feel proud to be of interest to such a highly regarded and esteemed gentleman. She only tries to forget a gentleman would never betray his wife.

Her eyes roam his perfect face, and she wonders not for the first time what he sees in Clara when he could have his pick of any wife. She seems so plain and dull, living in the shadow of her husband. Perhaps Annalise is the glue that binds them. Her trips to London with her mother gave them the opportunity to see one another but now Clara is home more. This makes their interludes less frequent but far more intense.

Elspeth is keener than ever to keep their relationship under wraps as she's already the talk of Bright Eye Lane thanks to Lilian and her escapades. That girl is a total enigma. She asked Garrison and Stevie to encourage her to return to the canteen at Whitworth's as her wayward ways were becoming a cause for concern to say the least. Poor Stevie, she leads him a merry dance. If it wasn't for him, she's sure Lilian would be out on the streets, because she would never come home again. Perhaps that's exactly what she needs: a short sharp shock to bring her back into the real world.

Garrison will sort it out Elspeth thinks, she can rely on him. She was lonely before he arrived on her doorstep one freezing December day, bearing a wreath of holly and a Christmas cake. The surprise of it will stay with her always and she found she looked forward to his visits more and more.

Then fate intervened yet again to move them along to another place.

Garrison called unexpectedly one Monday teatime when she'd just returned from Sissy's. She had been moaning about Samuel and Elspeth was short with her. Slumped in a chair by the fire, Elspeth was shedding a tear or two about the state of her daughters' lives. Where had she gone wrong? She couldn't fathom it when they had so much to be thankful for—Lilian had her freedom and Sissy had a husband who was a good provider and had given her two wonderful sons. Her grandsons are her joy, nothing less. Her girls used to be so close, bound more so by loss and grief but now it's as though they hate one another. Their father would be devastated were he still here.

When a knock came at the back door, she knew who it would be, and she almost didn't answer it. Perhaps it would have been better if she hadn't but somehow Elspeth couldn't help herself traipsing to the front door to unlock it. She was seeking the solace he could bring so she wouldn't have to face life's challenges feeling completely alone.

But more than that ... she wanted him.

She often laid awake imagining how it would be to be loved by Garrison, but this was only part of his attraction. It was at that precise moment she realised that rightly or wrongly she had fallen in love with Garrison Whitworth.

"What is it?" he asked. His face was full of concern but something else, something obvious to Clara.

He too had fallen in love with her.

She didn't want to explain, she only wanted to fall into his arms. He held her tightly as she wept softly

135

until her lips searched for his. His response was passionate as they kissed like young lovers snatching a stolen moment in an alleyway, feverish with desire for one another. Her hands slid down his back to his buttocks and his followed suit down her body, their lips still locked in their first kiss. Pulling away she almost pleaded, "Garrison, love me, love me in the way I've longed to be loved again."

Lifting her skirts, his fingers moved until she groaned into his neck; she reached the fastener of his trousers with fumbling hands. He was overcome with lust; so much so he almost reached the heights too quickly when he entered her. Elspeth's back was against the wall of the hallway, the sunshine flooding her face through the fanlight above the door. She looked to Garrison like a goddess as he fell deeper and deeper into her. He had never experienced such passion in his whole life and when he shuddered his love into her, he knew she had changed him.

Elspeth's love for Garrison is unexpected. With Frank it was a profound love but straightforward and traditional. In contrast, their love is borne from lust, longing, passion, all new yet no less satisfying than her marital love. She and Garrison 'play house' when he visits and for this stage of her life this is more appealing to her than marriage. She has the excitement and the companionship without the domestic mundanity, so for however long it lasts she has it all. She's not a silly, young girl, she knows their relationship must end one day. This little thought sits at the back of her mind sometimes more comfortably than others but it heightens the excitement. She likes to do her hair the way he likes, wear the scent he buys each Christmas and birthday and bask in the anticipation of their next liaison.

She would never accept any money from Garrison other than wages, though in truth she could do with more. Sissy still helps her out and her little job in the canteen is perfect, or it would be if Lilian returned to work. She's annoyed her mind has wandered to the girl; she's steadily become the fly in her ointment, spoiling each day.

She hears the latch lift on the gate. Dropping her spoon into the bowl with a clatter, her whole body stiffens. This is it she thinks and although she's never needed to do it before, she deftly sets the wheels of her plan in motion.

"Garrison," she whispers, whipping his bowl away and pressing his coat into his hands, "somebody is at the door. You must go out the back way—quickly!"

He's playing catch up with what she means as she ushers him down the narrow hallway. Then, Elspeth turns to see Lilian with her key in her hand, a strange smile on her face.

"Well, well, well, it seems you weren't quick enough, Mr Whitworth. How do you do this fine evening? Mam," Lilian says, inclining her head dramatically with a mock greeting.

A slight slurring of her words tells Elspeth her daughter has had more than one drink. She remembers Lilian had been dabbling with blackberry wine and now it seems something has driven her to the bottle.

What now, Elspeth wonders frozen to the spot.

Lilian tuts as Garrison joins her mother's side, the act of solidarity adding fuel to the fire. Her simmering anger is rapidly turning to fury.

"You've been a slippery little eel over the last few months, Mr Whitworth, by that you have. Given me the run around and no mistaking. Farmer Copley has waited long enough. He wants his rent or I'm out," Lilian says with the door still open.

Elspeth remembers the neighbours and rushes to the front door to close it, shooing Lilian into the kitchen.

"Now what have you come here for all in a tizzy; what's Mr Whitworth got to do with anything? He's asked you to come back to work time and time again but, oh no, working's beneath you now. You'd rather keep Stevie waiting and wondering, poor lad."

Garrison stays quiet. He knows any word from him whatever it may be will only stir the pot.

A loud hollow laugh escapes Lilian, startling her mother.

"Oh mother, you're a fine one to be lording it over me. Mr Whitworth hasn't just called in for a cup of tea and a bit of sponge cake, has he? Who are you to talk about my failings."

Turning to face Garrison, Lilian tilts her chin, squaring up to her nemesis.

"I've been to see your wife and now I'm here to see you. I thought this might be the place to find you."

Elspeth and Garrison exchange horrified glances whilst Lilian enjoys the sense of satisfaction a little pinch of power instils in her heart.

"So, I'll ask you for the first and last time: are you going to pay my rent?" she asks.

A shadow crosses Garrison's perfect face and his eyes glint in Lilian's direction. She's upset the applecart and by the look of her now she's thoroughly enjoying herself he thinks.

"What does she mean, Garrison?" Elspeth asks him, her heart racing in her chest.

"Tell her, Garrison why don't you?" Lilian says, sarcastically placing great emphasis on his first name, "Be my guest, I'm sick to the back teeth of all the deception. Let's all lay our cards out on the table and have a good look so we can get on with our lives."

"Don't," Garrison says, addressing Lilian, his tone somewhere between threatening and pleading, "remember the paper you signed."

"Now suddenly I have your full attention. Did you think I'd just come back to work with my tail between my legs? You owe me, you owe me and I'm calling it in."

"Lilian, you're frightening me now. What did you sign?" Elspeth asks.

Lilian pushes between them and heads to the back door.

"I'll leave you to explain, Garrison," she says, "Mad as I am at my mother, I can't hang about and watch."

Looking over her shoulder Lilian hesitates with her hand on the doorknob.

"Oh, and if my rent isn't paid by midday tomorrow, you'll leave me with no alternative but to finish what I've started and you know what that means."

She returns Garrison's look of pure contempt head on, free from fear and foreboding. The Dutch courage is serving her well.

"You would do well to remember I've got nothing to lose anymore," she tells him before slamming the door behind her.

Lilian heads down the street negotiating the cobbles as she goes. But with each step her anger steadily subsides to be replaced by regret. She feels a tear wetting her face, wiping it away quickly with the back of her hand. Oh, Lily, what have you done she thinks, her bottom lip starting to quiver like a broken butterfly wing.

Tonight, my mother's heart will be broken, utterly broken.

And I am the culprit.

Chapter 20

1897—Annalise

How can it be? Six weeks ago, my life was perfect in my eyes and now I'm sitting with a husband who has cheated death but barely.

Some of his speech has returned following the surgery but it can take minutes for him to say one sentence which is beyond frustrating for someone as articulate as Hugo and his right hand remains of little use.

"Will he improve?" I asked Dr Lloyd a week ago.

I wanted to say, "Will I ever have my husband back?" but the answer terrified me.

"Mrs Harper, with your care and devotion, anything is possible. You make a wonderful nurse."

He was humouring me to evade the question but perhaps it's impossible for him to know because there is no definitive treatment for apoplexy. Dr Lloyd says the prognosis and outcome is different for every individual and has advised rest, gentle massage for his affected hand and under no circumstances any distress.

For five days I laid on top of the bedspread by Hugo's side. Each morning when I woke, I braced myself for him not being with me any longer. I have never known a fear like it, as though your very world could be crushed to dust and scattered to the four winds at any moment. The trauma still follows me.

Now Hugo not only looks different, but he also smells different, acts differently and I find myself having to dig deep and search my soul to find love for this stranger.

"Oh, why don't you up sticks to London and be done with it?" Hugo asked me, his face contorted with exasperation when he couldn't use his spoon, "I give you a free pass to get out of here while you're still young enough to find somebody else."

I quickly reminded myself this wasn't Hugo talking, it was only his frustration.

"My darling, I'm going nowhere," I told him, "In sickness and in health was the vow I made, and I meant it."

His face crumpled and I held him as he sobbed into my chest like a small child. I'd never seen my husband cry before, but then what was there to cry about before this living nightmare?

The guilt got a grip when I realised it was like holding a person who had fallen on the street. Like I didn't know them, but I wanted to provide comfort as one human being to another. I'm so sorry, Hugo, forgive me I thought as I rocked him.

Mama and papa have been marvellous, calling every single day without fail and I count down the minutes to their arrival.

"Well, every cloud has a silver lining so they say," papa said, "I can't deny how much I'm enjoying having you home more."

Mama smiled and patted his hand saying, "And you too, my dear. It's wonderful to see more of you, isn't it Annalise?"

I smiled ruefully.

"It is, indeed, mama. Now, if you don't mind, I must bundle you two lovestruck young things out the door as I have things I must attend to."

Their affection made me uncomfortable for the first time. I thought of the Hugo of old, longed for him, his gentle touches, caresses. He always knew what I was thinking before I expressed it and even though we often had differing opinions our debates were a fascinating insight into my husband's mind, the mind of a talented writer.

I think of one of our conversations before all this.

"No, I will never ride on the back of your glory, Annalise," he insisted, when I suggested he might wish to use my good fortune to promote his work. If I can't make it as an author under my own steam, then so be it."

I was laying on his chest whilst he played with a lock of my hair with one hand and smoked a cigarette with the other. We were in what I thought of as *our* bed at the *Hotel Cecil*. We'd arrived back late from an after party where he'd been tantalising me all evening, running his fingertips up and down my back when nobody was looking. He had even dared to let his hand wander up my skirts in the carriage home, making me pulsate with anticipation. We were both so eager to fall into bed that night.

I lifted my head to look at him.

"You're shooting yourself in the foot, Hugo. I would only be opening the door, the rest would be up to you. I think it a shame the world cannot know what a fine writer you are."

He let out a theatrical sigh, rolling me onto my back then kissing my neck.

"Then perhaps I'm destined to remain a tortured author for the rest of my days. Perhaps the artistic struggle is the lure for me."

I laughed until he ran his tongue over my nipple and then trailed warm kisses down my stomach coming to a halt between my thighs. Oh, the memory is too much, and I wonder if I will ever share such moments with my husband again.

Last night I received a telegram from Howie inviting himself to stay for a night or perhaps two, this sending the house into a flurry of activity to be fit for his arrival.

How I've missed the companionship of my friend. Our easy banter is something I've come to cherish even more in his absence.

I couldn't be more pleased to see him when Sutcliffe finally announces his arrival. Howie rushes to kiss my hand before splitting his coat tails to sit down. Staring at his kindly face flooded with compassion I press a handkerchief to my mouth to smother a wail. He leans forward to pat my arm.

"Well, if this is the effect that I have on you I shall return to London on the next train," he says with a gentle smile.

"I apologise for the histrionics, Howie. I appear to have lost my stoicism suddenly."

Feeling foolish, I turn my attention to pouring the tea to try and compose myself.

"The great British stiff upper lip can be your enemy as much as your friend, in my opinion. It's very overrated," he says.

I hand him his teacup saying, "This is why I've missed you so much, you always know what to say."

"May I see Hugo soon?" he asks, taking a piece of shortbread.

My hand flutters to my throat.

"I'm afraid Hugo isn't keen to receive visitors in his vulnerable state as he calls it. I hope you don't mind, Howie."

"Mind? I would feel entirely the same in his position, you know how vain I can be. Oh well, I suppose I can put up with you for a day or two if I must," he says, shaking his head.

Hysterical laughter escapes me startling both of us before the sound swiftly changes to a sob.

As Howie falls at my feet, I lose track of time so I've no idea how long he holds me in his arms.

But I know I will never forget the comfort I feel in this moment.

*

I mouth a goodnight to Howie before opening my bedroom door. I've been three times to see Hugo throughout the day and helped him with the rigorous exercise regime set by Dr Lloyd. Some he can do alone but for others he needs me. It can be tiring, and I know Sutcliffe would be a good substitute, but I want Hugo to know he can lean on me. I've seen signs of improvement and cling to the hope that time is all it will take to make him better.

Time and patience.

"I see you've decided to grace me with your presence," Hugo says.

I thought he would be asleep so I'm not ready for the churlish comment. I'm so weary and I only want to fall into bed and draw a line under the day.

"Hugo, you know we have a houseguest, and I must play hostess. Howie has entertained himself in the library and walked the grounds whilst I've been with you. With his low boredom threshold, I think he's been very accommodating."

I laugh gently in the hope of placating him.

"I'd appreciate it if you didn't speak to me like a child, Annalise," he spits.

This is his illness talking I remind myself yet again though it's wearing thin. Walking to the dressing table I sit down to take the pins from my hair. I can't remember when I last had a proper night's sleep because I never know what will happen during the night. Will he call out with pain or distress; will he reach for me to hold him or sleep like a baton of wood at my side? Sleep eludes me and today is the first day I haven't felt alone in weeks. I'm filled with self-reproach at the thought and lower my eyes from Hugo's gaze in the mirror.

"Have you had a jolly old time with your *friend* this evening?" he asks.

The emphasis on the word 'friend' isn't lost on me.

"Yes, it's been nice to see him again and he's most concerned about you, my love."

Rolling his eyes towards the ceiling he lays silent a moment. I brush my hair slowly, delaying getting into bed as he's in this sullen mood.

"I don't think he's that concerned about me. He's always held a candle for you, everybody knows it," he says sulkily.

Spinning around in my seat, my mouth drops slightly at the comment.

"Howie has been a dear friend to both of us and we owe him a great deal," I say struggling to keep my voice level for so many reasons.

I deliberately avoid a response to his suggestion that Howie is anything other than a patron and confidante.

I watch a tear roll down the side of his face as he turns his head my way.

"Well, with me indisposed, I could hardly blame you for seeking solace elsewhere, Annalise."

Running towards the bed I jump to land beside him on my knees. I can't bear it. The sadness, the desolation in his voice is too much. For the first time in so long I feel genuine affection and compassion. To be laid hour upon hour with such thoughts must be torture.

Taking his face between both my palms I kiss his crooked mouth lightly.

"My darling Hugo," I tell him as I raise my head from our kiss, my eyes boring into his, "I care nothing for solace from Howie or anyone else."

"You say that now but …"

Placing my hand to his mouth I stop his train of words before they hurtle off the track. The damage they may inflict is not necessary.

"You must be rid of this thought, Hugo, or it will drive you to misery and madness."

Nodding his head, he touches my cheek, and my throat tightens. I know I hold the key to salve his pain once and for all though I will be betraying a confidence. But as his wife it's my duty to ease his pain surely, I decide.

I take a deep breath.

"In any case, Howie of all people is the least of your worries."

Hugo shakes his head wondering what I am referring to.

"He has, how to put it, a particular taste in love. I'm of no interest to him whatsoever though I'm trusting you with a secret of some magnitude. I know I can trust you."

Now it has become my husband's turn to drop his mouth agape with surprise.

Chapter 21

1897—Sissy

Sissy watches her sister staggering towards her, head down. She can tell Lilian is concentrating hard to walk in a straight line but it's patently obvious she's drunk.

Should she walk on by if Lilian doesn't lift her head and notice her, she wonders. It would be in both their best interests. Somewhat irritatingly, her conscience makes the decision for her.

"Lily, have you been to see mam?" she asks, touching her arm briefly.

The glaze of Lilian's eyes turns to a cloud of contempt when she realises it's her sister. Her eyes don't light up when she sees her at the best of times and judging by the filthy streaks on her face, this is anything but.

"Oh, you needn't wrinkle your nose so much at me, Sis, I know I've had a drink or two but at least I'll be sober in the morning. What's your excuse for looking so miserable every day of your life, eh?"

Sissy sees the curtain move at number eight. Mrs Jarvis peers around and this prompts her to swiftly guide Lilian by her elbow to the side of the privy.

"Oy, get off me," Lilian says before stumbling back to lean against the wall with her arms folded.

She can see Whitworth's brass lettering over Sissy's shoulder which makes her think of the day she told Stevie about the baby. They were more or less in this very same spot. The fight suddenly goes out of her, and she drops her arms.

"Did you know about mam?" Lilian asks.

Sissy flops back against the wall at the side of her sister, hanging her head.

"Yes of course, everybody knows. Mam thinks they're being so clever using the ginnel, but this is a small street with next to no privacy. I can't believe she doesn't know she's the talk of it. I suppose she'll be in denial so she can still hold her head up when she walks past the neighbours."

Lilian turns her head and stares at her sister.

"That bugger wants it all: a wife, child, mistress, a fortune. All he had to do was pay for my rent, that's all I asked in return for sealing his happiness."

Sissy isn't listening because she's only just become aware of something—something very distasteful.

"Our mam is a mistress," she states flatly, raising her eyes to look at Lilian.

Lilian looks away and swallows saying, "Don't say that. I can't think of her as that."

The wind blows their fringes from their faces making them look like a pair of bookends as they stare straight ahead deep in thought. Though they may look alike, the similarities end there.

"Have you only just found out?" Sissy asks.

"I've known a while but kept it to myself. When he wouldn't play ball with the rent, I was forced to confront his wife," Lilian tells her, "Guess what though, it turns out she already knew."

Sissy's face hangs with astonishment.

"She knew; what kind of woman turns a blind eye to that kind of lying and deception?"

She thinks of Samuel and wonders if she's turning a blind eye to his lying and deceit. If she is, if any other woman wants him, they can have him Sissy thinks, all my prayers would be answered.

"I don't know, it's beyond me. Garrison Whitworth has been playing all of us and he thought I would back down and just do as I'm told. He knows mam wants me to be like everybody else and he wants mam to have what she wants."

Sissy whips her head in her sister's direction suddenly irritated.

"She's not alone in that way of thinking. For god's sake, Lily, just *be* like everybody else and go to work. Why should you be different, why should you be special when we all must do things we don't want to? We all have a cross to bear."

Lilian's face flushes with fury; she's sick of hearing it. Who the hell does she think she is talking to me like that, she thinks, she's not my bloody mother.

"Oh, we all know about your crosses, don't we just!" Lilian shouts, "If it isn't Samuel then it's me—it's never you Sissy, never. You want it all just like Garrison Whitworth and if he doesn't do as I ask, he'll be sorry and so will you."

Lilian starts backing away down the ginnel.

"What do you mean by that?" Sissy asks walking towards her.

"I mean that the truth must come out one way or another … for everybody."

Grabbing hold of the collar of Lilian's dress Sissy hisses, "If you do that then it will finish us all. Mam's reputation will be ruined, and you'll break that young lass's heart if she finds out the truth. You've lost your bloody mind; I can't have it I tell you."

Lilian slaps Sissy's hand away and straightens the collar of her dress. She has the power over all of them, and she knows it. How dearly Sissy would love to swipe that smug smile clean off her sister's face.

"Everything alright, you two?" Stevie asks, appearing at the end of the privy ginnel.

The sisters look startled, but Lilian composes herself first.

"Fine, Stevie, fine, we're just catching up," she says.

He looks between them both for clues.

"I've got a bit of brisket for tea, Lily if you're ready for home," he says, never taking his eyes of them.

"Oh, lovely, thanks Stevie," Lilian says, "We'll be off then Sissy, see you soon."

Lilian throws a sickly smile at Sissy over her shoulder and takes Stevie's arm.

Sissy watches them until they disappear from the street, thinking it will a cold day in hell before she will let her wayward sister get everything she wants.

Now after the show they've made of themselves, she takes the long walk of shame back down Bright Eye Lane back to what she thinks of as her poor excuse of a home ... and a life.

Chapter 22

1897—Stevie

He didn't mean to watch her. He reminds himself often he's not some peeping tom, quite the opposite in fact. Stevie is a gentleman; everybody says so and he prides himself on it.

So, when he found himself staring down into the kitchen of number two, though he'd never been to the theatre, he imagined it was like watching a scene from a play. The scene changed daily, and the characters' lives unfolded before his eyes, but they were unaware of being watched. They were free, uninhibited, and even though he couldn't hear the words they were saying he could guess them from their body language. It all came about purely by accident.

Sissy was sweet on him at school, but he had never encouraged her or lead her on when they left. Then Samuel caught her eye, and her future was decided. He didn't care because he only had eyes for one woman and Stevie is definitely a one-woman man. She'd lived in that house her whole life. The nets start halfway down the sash window so the family couldn't be seen from the yard, but he had a front row seat from the upper floor to their little domestic drama and he made sure he wasn't seen. Some days he couldn't tear himself away from his watch post in the storeroom. The women were beautiful, fascinating, captivating and he couldn't help but fall in love.

The orange glow of lamplight bathed the cosy parlour. This was a place of chats around the table or the fireside. He saw laughter and tears throughout the years but mostly he watched the mundane. He liked the way they took it in turns to do the dishes and hang the washing on the pully rail over the fire every Monday without fail in winter. He liked the way the girls kissed their mother when they came home from work and the way she caressed their cheek briefly with the lightest of touches. They took it for granted but he never had the touch of his mother or if he did, he couldn't remember it. In the summertime the window was often open, and the snowy nets billowed in the breeze creating an ethereal frame to the scene.

Sometimes his throat caught, and he had an ache that was almost a pain in his chest. Stevie had a longing, a yearning even, just to be part of that family.

Then one day he received what he could only describe as a body blow. He felt tears burn his eyes as his personal drama became sullied. Stevie turned and walked away from the window in disgust. And Garrison Whitworth, his mentor, was responsible. The shock of discovering the truth and seeing people he had held in high esteem topple from their pedestals was hard to bear and affected him badly for a very long time.

Yet still the love remained.

Of all people, why did it have to be Garrison who ruined his dream? He loved Garrison like a father. He'd turned to him when Lilian got into trouble, he'd come to their rescue in miraculous fashion, so it was somehow so much worse that it was him.

At first, he tried to hate Elspeth but soon realised she had done nothing wrong to him and even if she had he would never be able to hate her. She was a beautiful young widow who was lonely. He knew she was lonely because she spent many an hour weeping or simply staring into the fire in the darkness. This was understandable when she first lost her husband but as time went on, he knew it wasn't good for her. He continued to call weekly with her wood haul even after Sissy and Lilian left but he made an excuse not to stay for tea and cake because he was tongue-tied and awkward around her, unsure what to say. So, he made a vow to look after her in other ways.

Stevie didn't worry about Sissy, she was strong and pragmatic, but he did worry about Lilian. He would have married her for Elspeth's sake but that would never be on the cards for Lilian, and he's come to accept it. He knows it's for the best as his heart lays elsewhere, and it's set in stone, an unmovable object. Lilian won't accept his money either because she has her pride and principles, and to her, this would make her a kept woman. Lilian is not a woman to be kept.

Today he saw the sisters rowing in the ginnel by the privy and it seemed to be getting out of hand. This was after he'd watched Lilian storming out of number two and Garrison leaving the house not too long afterwards. Elspeth's face was contorted with anger but also something else: distress, Stevie realised.

This time he couldn't just stand by and watch so he intervened, took Lily home and made her tea. They ate in silence by the fire, neither of them wanting to speak for different reasons. His mind was elsewhere; he'd found out the reason for the drama on the way home and he wanted to leave, he didn't want to be part of it. When Lilian fell into a drunken sleep, he left a note to tell her he would see her the following day and slipped out of the cottage.

Now, making a detour to Bright Eye Lane he stands outside the tall gate to the yard of number two. He can just see the light from the kitchen as he paces the frosted flags unsure if he has the nerve to knock on the door. What's the alternative he wonders, going home to lay awake with the thought of Elspeth Reid sitting alone in her kitchen filled with despair?

When he knocks on the door, he has the urge to run away like a child, like the night he knocked on Garrison's door, but tonight he decides he must be a man. He has to knock three times as she will be in no mood for visitors. He must hold fast to his nerve.

"Stevie!" Elspeth exclaims as she pulls the door back.

Did he imagine the brief shadow of disappointment crossing her pale face he wonders?

"I'm sorry to disturb you at this hour, Mrs Reid but Lilian has … has put me in the picture about what went on this afternoon."

"I see," she says wearily, "You'd better come in, I'd rather not air my smalls on the doorstep."

Tucking a stray wisp of hair behind her ear she stands back to allow him entry to her cosy little home. She nods to his usual spot at the table, and he sits down and plays with his cap. The room is cold as the fire is low and he feels a stranger in a house he has visited weekly for many a year.

"I suppose you're disgusted in my behaviour," she says laying the kettle on the coals after broddling the flames to life.

"I'm not here to go into all that, I only want to check if you're alright after your shock."

Elspeth looks at the red-haired man sitting at her table as if for the first time. When did he become a man? She thought. She'd always thought of him as a boy, a youngster like her daughters. It's the wrong question to ask Elspeth with such a note of compassion in his voice at this moment. Her face crumples.

"As you ask, I'm not really alright, Stevie," she says, plonking herself opposite him at the table. Laying her head on her forearm he's startled when a loud sob escapes her.

Now he's not sure what to do. He reaches to touch her hand but then pulls away until another sob echoes in the quietness of the room. This time he lightly touches her hand, and she grabs his fingers and clings to them like she's on hanging on for grim death.

"Oh, Stevie," she says, "how could she? That was my granddaughter, I could have helped her," her hold tightens on his hand, "What went wrong with Lilian, I don't understand?"

"She isn't a bad lass, Mrs Reid," Stevie says earnestly, feeling the need to spring to Lilian's defence, "she just doesn't like people very much. All she wants is to live a simple life of on her own, a life where she's free and not bogged down by the rules of society."

Elspeth looks up into Stevie's gentle eyes, a wry smile tilting her lips. Stevie couldn't be happier to see it.

"She was always a tomboy wasn't she, always a little wild compared to Sissy, if you remember?" she says.

He's still holding her hand he notices, and she doesn't even attempt to pull away.

"All that went on back then is bad enough but then for Garrison to betray me all these years, it's too much I tell you."

A tear hurtles down her face to fall from her chin. He'd like to pull her into his arms. The urge is so instinctive he almost does, but he's taken aback when she quickly pulls her had from his.

"Stevie, tell me honestly why you're here tonight," she pauses, her face flushed and frantic, "Are you here because you're the father of the child?" she asks, her eyes great circles of realisation.

He can feel his mouth open and close more than once as she stares at him. What to say; Lilian has never disclosed who Annalise's real father is, not even to him. This will break, Elspeth he thinks. If she's led to believe her daughter is not only wild but flighty, a loose woman, it will be her undoing.

He listens to the tap dripping into the bowl in the sink trying to get the words to come out of his mouth.

When he finally succeeds, all hope of any connection with Elspeth, real or fantasy is lost because he can only nod his head once then lower it too upset to look at her.

Stevie feels a burning shame; a shame which isn't even his to burn with.

Chapter 23

1898—Annalise

"Wait there a moment," Hugo says.

I glance at mama who raises her eyebrows as papa puts his brandy glass down on the side table with anticipation.

"What is it, dear?" I ask struggling to keep my even tone.

Mama senses I'm drained and all set for bed, not up to any revelations or excitement. Papa is oblivious looking between us all with ruddy cheeks.

To think I was bored and restless not so long ago. The days stretched out like an endless sky not helped by my mind being too preoccupied to settle on any hobby. Hugo was improving daily and was even sitting up in bed to read by then so he demanded less of my time. We continued with the exercises, and I called in often to see him, but the time dragged in between.

One morning I came downstairs from having breakfast in our room when I saw Sutcliffe paying the coalman at the back door. How long it seemed since we'd had any visitors other than my parents and Howie. I tried to think how long exactly when my mind went to the day Hugo took ill. I was compelled to ask the question.

"Sutcliffe, on the day I was summoned to return from London we had a knock on the door from an unexpected visitor; can you recall who it was?" I said.

Pausing mid step in the hallway, Sutcliffe glances upwards trying to remember.

"Ah, yes, a woman by the name of Reid and she was visiting from High not too far from your father's house," he said nodding. Sutcliffe's ability to recall people and events was quite remarkable but a valuable trait in a butler.

"Will that be all madam," he asked, jolting me from the memory of that terrible day.

I'm not quite satisfied.

"I wonder what she could possibly have wanted?"

"Well, she never returned so it can't have been too important," Sutcliffe said, "Will there be anything else, madam?"

I wanted to say, yes, come with me into the parlour so we can have a chat or a game of chess but that would of course have been entirely inappropriate. I shook my head and thanked him, and he left me to continue his tasks.

I mooched alone into the parlour and stared out of the window. I was doing too much of that in those days. How I missed London, my freedom, even the hotel. Boredom is like an ache, and I was reminded of my childhood.

The mysterious visitor plagued my thoughts all day. If I'd been busy perhaps it might not have been the same but by the following morning, I could stand it no longer.

After breakfast I summoned Sutcliffe to ask him to organise the carriage and instructed Burton to take me to Haigh .

I popped my head around the door to tell Hugo of my intentions and though he was a little perplexed about why it was so important, he didn't make a fuss and I assured him I'd be back in plenty of time for dinner.

"I will look forward to hearing all about your investigations on your return, Mr Holmes," he said, and I laughed, happy to see another little glimpse of the old Hugo.

How wonderful it was to have meaning to my day after so long. As we reached the open countryside I hung out of the window and filled my lungs with the fresh air, immediately feeling more myself.

I had no idea how we would find the woman, but Haigh was only a small hamlet so when we arrived, I asked Burton to enquire at the blacksmiths.

|We were directed to a dirt track about a quarter mile along the road at the end of which I could see what could only be described as a semi-derelict farmhouse. At the front of the building sat an older woman in a shabby overcoat looking taken aback when she saw the carriage approaching as if from nowhere.

"Good afternoon, madam," I said from the carriage window, "I wonder if you might be able to help me."

She came to end of the path, a headscarf tied under her chin and wearing boots caked in mud.

"If I can, I will, miss," she said cheerily, leaning her thick set body on the gate.

I found the title amusing; the woman obviously thought I was younger than I am.

"Thank you. Well, to explain, I'm trying to locate the whereabouts of an acquaintance of mine who I haven't seen for some time. The name is Reid. I hoped that my white lie would put the old woman at her ease and less inclined to view me with suspicion.

For a moment she said nothing but then she must have decided she could trust me saying, "I can only think you mean Lilian Reid – she's a tenant on our land. You'll find her about a mile down yonder."

She pointed her grubby finger down the track and beyond the farmhouse.

"I'm grateful to you," I said then.

The woman lifted her hand to make a cursory wave as we carried on our way, and I realised with some sadness how removed I had become from the village life I had known as a girl. I missed that.

The little cottage was rather ramshackle but charming in its own way and I found myself wondering if Lilian lived there alone or with a husband because it was quite remote.

After knocking a few times without an answer, I decided we should wait a while so I stroked the horses instead and listened to Burton telling me how he looked after them.

We must have waited around twenty minutes or so when a lady with dark hair and a basket appeared from around the rear of the cottage. Stopping in her tracks when she saw us, she stood staring without a word or greeting until I spoke.

"Are you Mrs Lilian Reid by any chance?" I asked, stepping forward.

She seemed to be considering her response for a while to what was a very straightforward question.

"I am," is all she said finally. She didn't go on to ask who I was or the nature of my visit. I felt unwelcome.

"I hope you'll forgive the intrusion but some time ago I think you might have called at my home, Sutton Manor, asking to see me, but I was indisposed at the time. It was so out of the blue and it must have been important for you to have travelled all that way. It has been preying on my mind so I thought I might try and find you to ask how I could help."

I was prattling. I was uncomfortable under her steady gaze.

Lilian Reid was very attractive if a little unkempt and windblown. She made no attempt to tidy her appearance and it occurred to me that perhaps visitors were a rare occurrence round these parts.

"Do you recall?" I asked eventually.

The silence hung between us with only birdsong to swallow it. I was unsure what to do or say next.

"Of course, yes, I remember now," she said, nodding her head, and seeming to come around from her stupor, "I ... I came to ask if you had any housekeeping vacancies at the manor. I'm no longer in need of a situation now though as my circumstances have since changed."

I sensed her discomfort but although I was desperate to press her further, I decided it wasn't the right thing to do.

Instead, smiling I said, "Ah, I see, mystery solved then. Well, I shall leave you to your afternoon, I'm sure you have plenty to do. Good day to you," I said inclining my head then making my way to return to the carriage. Burton immediately scrambled down to help me.

"Wait, please," she almost shouted, "Where are my manners; would you care for a cup of tea before you resume your journey?"

The last part was said in a voice which sounded affected, perhaps trying to enunciate her words more clearly. I found it quite sweet of her to bother.

"That would be most welcome," I said, glad of the opportunity to pursue my detective work.

"Annelise Harper," I said, not forgetting the simple courtesies when one is visiting.

She smiled but barely then I followed her down the path and she dropped her basket at the doorway. It was full of herbs of some description and leaves which looked like nettles. I couldn't help smiling inwardly at the notion of her being a witch. Was it safe to follow her inside? I knew nothing of this woman, she was a total stranger. I chided myself for my overactive imagination. Perhaps I was on my way to going stir crazy I thought.

Once inside the cottage my eyes discreetly roamed the tiny room which seemed to house everything but a bed. To think she lived, cooked and slept in this one room which was just as unkempt as its owner, but warm and homely.

I told her as much as she plumped the cushion of the seat by the fire.

"Perhaps decaying and crumbling might be a more fitting description," she said.

Our eyes met and we shared a small laugh. It went some way in putting us both more at ease I could tell.

She made tea and then left the house with a tray for Burton. I heard him thank her warmly then she said, "You're welcome, no doubt you'll be parched after your journey."

Then when she came back inside, she settled herself opposite me and we exchanged a little about our lives.

"So, you grew up on the same street as Whitworth's and you mother works there?" I asked.

"How uncanny, that happens to be my father's business," I said.

She smiled for no apparent reason but didn't respond.

"How wonderful it must be to be a famous opera singer," Lilian said suddenly taking me unawares.

I wondered how she could know, and my face must have betrayed my thoughts as she quickly explained her mother knew a little about my life from working at Whitworth's.

Embarrassed, I lowered my head and shook it. I didn't want her to think I had ideas above my station; somehow, I wanted her to like me.

"I suppose I have gained a name for myself in certain circles, but my life has changed dramatically of late as my husband has been unwell."

"Oh, I'm sorry. I hope he's getting better," she said.

Was it the way Lilian said it or her compassionate expression that made my throat catch I wondered afterwards. Her eyes were clear pools of concern and I had to look away quickly.

"Thank you, he's improving slowly. It's been quite a worrying time and there was a moment when I thought I'd ... I'd lost him," I said my voice cracking on the last words.

Lilian stayed silent but our eyes locked and held. We seemed to be communicating without words and it was so profound.

"Oh dear, here am I getting all upset when you were no doubt planning a peaceful afternoon in your sweet little cottage. I'm sorry, I suppose I haven't been able to speak to anyone properly about it for some time. I don't say much to mama as she does worry so."

"You've nothing to apologise for ..."

She didn't get time to finish because just then the door opened and in walked a beautiful lady of mature years. She had the same colouring as Lilian, and I knew who she was immediately. She took a step back, her mouth widening into almost a circle though she must have seen the carriage to know Lilian had a visitor. Perhaps she realised who I was from working at Whitworth's.

"Mrs Harper, this is my mother, Elspeth Reid," Lilian said quickly.

"Annalise, please. Good afternoon, Mrs Reid, I'm afraid I landed on your daughter's doorstep unexpectedly," I said.

Lilian interjects saying, "No matter, you're only returning the favour. It's exactly what I did to you last year."

Lilian's voice trailed away to a nervous laugh and her mother turned from her to smile my way.

"I'm very happy to make your acquaintance, Annalise, I'm sure. Please, do call me Elspeth."

We took each other's hands and Elspeth covered them with her free hand. I could almost feel the warmth and kindness of the lady in just that fleeting moment.

"Well, I must be on my way. Thank you for your hospitality," I said to Lilian.

"Please don't go on my account," Elspeth said, "I would love us to enjoy a cup of tea by the fire if you have the time."

My eyes went to Lilian who was smiling and nodding her head. I was utterly charmed into submission by the pair.

So, Lilian went outside with more refreshments for Burton, and I spent another hour in their company. It was such a pleasant afternoon and we dropped Elspeth home in the carriage on our way back to Sutton Manor.

After Burton helped her down, Elspeth turned and looked at me through the window. Her daughter is the image of her I noticed.

"Goodness knows what people will say," she said, gesturing towards the carriage.

"It's the least I can do in return for you and Lilian's hospitality," I replied.

"I hope you don't think me forward," she said shyly, "but I call at Lilian's every Saturday afternoon. Would you care to visit us again next week?"

I was both taken aback and delighted. The women had indeed been the tonic I needed, and I felt invigorated after our little gathering. I was perplexed at first to why they wished to spend time with me, but I was happy to know they must have felt the same.

Undeterred, I made the return journey the following week, collecting Elspeth from number two Bright Eye Lane. We chatted like old friends on route to Lilian's cottage and I received a warm welcome when we got there. It's become a weekly routine and I look forward to it immensely.

Now Hugo takes my breath away when he suddenly gets to his feet and stands holding the cane which has become a part of him over the months. I want to shout out when he turns to hang the cane on the back of the armchair and stands unaided. I expect him to fall back into the chair any second and jump up from my seat with agitation.

Holding up his hand to stop me going any further he takes six faltering steps to cover the distance between us. I'm overcome. Tears flow freely from both of us and I wrap my arms around my husband, feeling his diminished frame. Now though he can build himself up day by day and I can be right by his side as he does it.

He's almost come back to me; my Hugo is on his way home.

"Oh, my darling, I'm so happy for you, for both of us," I say.

"Well, I won't be climbing mountains any time soon, but I never was one for the great outdoors."

Laughing together my heart sings. We're on the right path, mountains can wait forever for me.

"Wait until I tell Lilian and Elspeth, they will be delighted," I say clasping my hands together. Saturday cannot come quick enough.

"Lilian and Elspeth?" Papa asks.

I'd almost forgotten he and mama were in the room.

"Yes, my new friends in Haigh. I thought mama would have told you as she and Hugo have heard so much about them over the last few months. They've been such a huge support, and I so look forward to our weekly get togethers. Elspeth works in the canteen, I'm certain you will know her."

Chapter 24

1898—Elspeth

"Quite the merry little troupe you've become," Sissy says, handing Elspeth the plate to dry.

Elspeth sighs but silently, realising she often does this when she's around her daughters.

"Sissy how is it you make everything sound so unseemly with your sarcastic tone? Yes, we have become friendly and there's no reason why you shouldn't join us from time to time," her mother says.

Rubbing the plate too vigorously in the soap suds, Sissy snaps, "Chance would be a fine thing. It's not long since I found out."

Elspeth wants to say that it's her own doing because she keeps her mother and sister at arm's length. She's not up to the drama today though, so instead she laughs, telling Sissy she'll rub the pattern off the plate if she's not careful.

Sissy's shoulders slump over the sink and for once Elspeth feels sorry for her.

"I'm excluded from everything with you and our Lily, I'm always finding out things third hand."

Elspeth considers her words for a moment. Sometimes a mother must be cruel to be kind and some well-placed home truths don't go amiss on occasion she decides.

"My dear, is it that you are excluded or is it that you exclude yourself? Bitterness is a terrible affliction and so caustic to one's heart," she says hanging up the tea towel on the door of the range to dry.

Sissy spins around from the sink, eyes flashing.

"Listen to yourself, always getting above yourself with your hoity toity words. You've been spending too much time around the high and mighty. You and Lilian are in cahoots, like two peas in a pod suddenly. Time was when you were as furious as me with her for her feral ways. Now, you're never away from the cottage. I don't know how you can look that girl in the face after what went on with … with her father."

Elspeth faces her daughter head on, eye to eye. For the first time in her life, she'd like to strike her but manages to stop herself in time. She's breathing heavily, struggling to get control of temper.

"Now look here, lady, I'll not overlook a chance to spend time with my granddaughter whatever the circumstances. As for the situation with her father, that's none of your business. You've no idea about loneliness and I wasn't the one who was married."

Elspeth expects Sissy to have plenty to say for herself, but she's horrified when her daughter bursts into tears. Elspeth slides her arm around her shoulders to guide Sissy to toward the table, sitting her down gently. She pours some more tea for them both, putting in an extra spoon of sugar to help with the shock just like her own mother told her to do when she was a child. She offers Sissy a handkerchief and she takes it to dab her face, then blows out a long, unsteady breath.

"That's it, lass, let it out, you don't do it often enough," Elspeth says.

"How can I mam when nobody listens to me? Just because Samuel doesn't beat me black, and blue doesn't make a difference to my mind. He's changed me over the years, made me the bitter person I am because I see you and our Lily running free. I might as well tell you now that our Lily was going to rent a place on the street with me, but she backed out at the last minute. I just can't forgive her for preventing me from escaping my life of misery."

Elspeth slumps back in her chair. She'd no idea Lilian had let her down in such a fashion. No wonder Sissy is bristling with resentment, it explains so much.

"Why didn't you ask to move in with me if he was so bad? I would have taken you in, make no bones about it," Elspeth says.

Sissy runs a hand down her face, shaking her head furiously with exasperation.

"Because you made me feel it was my fault that I couldn't make my marriage work. I didn't want to come to live here feeling a failure, swapping one kind of misery for another. You were so happy with dada, so you can never understand. But Samuel's no dada I can tell you that much. Sometimes I think he's evil and I should do something drastic to rid the world of him but I'm too weak to even do that."

Tears appear in Elspeth's eyes as she stares at the top of her daughter's head. When did she start going grey; why hadn't she noticed? She's always been too busy worrying about Lilian to take any notice of her eldest child. She's just had her down as a moaner, somebody who was never satisfied.

"I'm sorry love, I should have taken your worries more seriously. It's me who's failed you."

Sissy doesn't speak, only making Elspeth feel worse.

"It's not too late though, why don't you move in now? The boys have left so it will just be the two of us."

Sniffing, Sissy attempts a smile.

"I'll think about it," she says.

But she couldn't move in here now after all that's gone on. I'm worth more than pity she thinks, I'll just have to wait and see if Samuel's cough gets worse like his mate, Harold's did. What a sorry state to wish my husband a dead man.

"Stevie will be here in a minute with the wood," Elspeth says getting up to wash the teacups, "I don't know, if Lilian had just married him when she had the chance there'd be none of this. They could have been a nice little family and he'd have made a smashing father."

Sissy jumps up and pulls her mother's arm to swing her around from the sink.

"Stevie, the father of the baby; is that what our Lily told you?"

"No, he told me himself after some persuading," Elspeth says, her eyes narrowing.

She's not sure what Sissy is getting at with this line of questioning and her peculiar smile is unnerving.

"For god's sake, Stevie isn't the father, mam, "Sissy says, "He was just protecting our Lily … and protecting you most likely."

Elspeth has no idea who or what to believe any longer. All this deceit is like wading through treacle, the lies wrapping an impenetrable slew around the truth.

"I don't understand, why would Stevie do such a thing, it doesn't make sense? Why on earth would he say he was the father when he isn't?" Elspeth asks, her hand clutching her chest.

Sissy drops her mother's arm then takes a step back.

"Look, it seems today is a day for revelations," she says, "Stevie loves our Lily alright but he's not in love with her. He loves her as a friend, that's all."

"How do you know all this, Sissy?"

"Mam, I've got eyes and ears like you, it's just I choose to use mine."

Elspeth stares at her daughter, her brow furrowing. She's full of questions but not sure if she should find out the answers.

"Look, there's no point in beating about the bush anymore. Stevie isn't in love with our Lily because he's in love with you. I doubt he's ever looked at another woman in the way he looks at you. I can't let him take the blame, it's just not right."

Stevie's in love with me, Elspeth thinks the words clear yet confusing; what in the world is Sissy wittering on about now, I'm old enough to be his mother.

The room swims as Elspeth grabs hold of the sink thinking there's nothing else for it, her daughter has finally snapped ... and lost her bloody mind.

*

With her parting shot Sissy lets herself out of the house.

Elspeth sits staring into the fire until she hears the gate go. Her heart plummets before she gets up to answer the door. What should I do; should I act normal; can I, she wonders?

Taking a deep breath, she opens the back door, a fake smile splitting her face. Stevie looks taken aback. Perhaps my expression is ghoulish enough to scare him she thinks.

"Come in out of the cold, lad," she says.

Piling the wood by the fire he stands with the empty basket in his hands. Elspeth is struck mute but somehow, she finds herself unable to tear her eyes away from the boy who's carried out this same weekly ritual for over two decades.

"Are you alright, Mrs Reid?" Stevie asks.

He's slightly chattier since the night he told her he was Annalise's father she realises as though he's trying to make it up to her. What a thing for the boy to do she thinks. Although his face is full of concern, she sees something more. Her throat is too tight. She's been prompted to take a proper look and she knows now what it is she sees. It's the same raw, unmistakable emotion she saw in Garrison's eyes that day.

He loves me, she thinks, he really and truly is in love me. The boy has wasted his entire adult life on a pipe dream.

Except Stevie is no longer a boy, he's a fully grown, strapping man. She's suddenly overcome with nerves and wishes she hadn't had the conversation with Sissy because now she's unable to be herself, unable to act normally.

"Sit down," Stevie says, "you look fit to drop. You've probably been doing too much. I'll get you a glass of water."

Sitting down he places the water in front of her and watches her intently as she sips.

It's no good, she must spit it out or it will choke her.

"Stevie, this is going to come as a shock, but I've found something out today."

His neck grows hot, so it will soon be covered with red blotches he thinks. Stevie's mind is firing in all directions, and he can't look Elspeth's way.

"You see, I have it on good authority that you're not actually Annalise's father."

The frank statement is not one he was prepared for. He swallows noisily then raises his eyes to sit quietly staring into the fire. He's never been one to overreact if she thinks about it. He's always been a steady, calm presence in the background; reliable, dependable. in all the years she'd known him.

"I'm sorry to blurt it out like that but I don't want you to keep up the pretence any longer."

He continues staring into the fire, unable to face her disappointment in him.

"No, well, I'm sorry I lied," he says, "I … I can only hope you can understand I did it for the right reasons."

Leaning forward she pats his hand. Stevie pulls away startled, like she's slapped him instead of the of the gentle touch she offered.

"My only concern is Lilian doesn't deserve such loyalty. I don't think you've been doing her or yourself any favours in cossetting her all these years."

Now Elspeth is the one who's startled as Stevie looks straight into her eyes. His face is taut as though she's offended him.

"You know, Lilian gets a bad press sometimes. She isn't a bad lass; she's got a big heart deep down. She's just too odd for people to look for it or even care. Her strange ways mean her kindness is overlooked because people can't see beyond them."

Elspeth eyes mist as she looks at the man who would defend her daughter's honour to the hilt. I am one of those people she thinks, the shame hurting her.

"Don't cry," is all he says.

Elspeth tries to swallow her tears, but one escapes to hurtle down her cheek.

"Stevie, I've made another discovery, one which took me even more by surprise. I know now you're not in love with Lilian and you're not in love with Sissy, though I think Sissy wishes you were."

Somehow, he manages to hold her gaze so long that his nerves ebb slightly. This is a 'now or never' moment in his life, he knows it without a shred of doubt.

"No, you're quite right, I'm ... I'm not in love with your daughters."

They continue to lock eyes, so his courage gathers momentum. Come on, Stephen, step up to the mark and show this woman what's really going on inside you, he thinks. You've nothing to lose as she knows anyway.

"I'm sorry you found out from Sissy about how I feel about you. I should have been man enough to tell you myself."

Still, they can't look away. Elspeth leans to take both Stevie's hands in hers and he holds on tightly, feeling the oddly wonderful coarseness of her palms. Her hands sum her up, he thinks, the backs of them white as snow, yet the palms telling the story of her hard life. Beautiful yet careworn, this is the story of Elspeth. This is why he loves her so.

"Sometimes the words just won't come no matter how hard we try, I understand that. I'm sorry you've wasted your life on me. I don't deserve it," she says.

He knows she's referring to Garrison with her last comment.

"Love isn't about perfection: if you're looking for that you'll fall at the first hurdle. I'm not perfect, nobody is. To me you have a heart of pure gold that's worthy of any love."

Such beautiful hidden depths. To think she might never have seen them; what a terrible loss.

"Stevie, I doubt it will have escaped your notice that I'm old enough to be your mother."

Shrugging he says, "And? As far as I know you always have been, and it's not made a blind bit of difference."

They're both surprised by his candidness. Stevie has well and truly strayed from his normal path. His hand has been forced but now there's no stopping him. It's his time, he knows it because he can feel it to his boots.

"Look, this is a shock, it's all new and odd for both of us. I don't want anything from you, nothing whatsoever. For my part, I can keep coming every week to bring you your wood and we can sit and have a cuppa and a slice of cake. I'd more than settle for that."

She reaches out to touch his face with her forefinger as though tracing the outline of it. The red hair, the strong jawline, they all look new. He was waiting in the wings all along and she didn't even see him until this very night.

An hour or more later she walks Stevie to the door, and they smile at each other. She loves him as a friend undoubtedly but wonders if she can love him as a woman loves a man. She knows he deserves such a love, nothing less and it brings her up short that she is even prepared to entertain the notion at all.

Perhaps she doesn't need to have the answer tonight, they can take all the time they need. He's waited this long.

Elspeth waits to wave to Stevie as he heads down the stone steps, empty wood basket in hand. Turning her way before he goes through the gate, he raises his free hand and throws her a half-smile, reminding her of their shared secret.

With a full mind she draws the curtains and dampens the fire with the leaves from the teapot. When she's heading up the stairs, she feels suddenly drained, keen to draw this remarkable day to a close.

But by the time Elspeth reaches the landing, one question lingers and she realises just how distracted she's been by the unexpected turn of events for the question to only occur to her just now:

So, if Stevie isn't Annalise's father, then who on earth is?

She makes to move across the landing towards her bedroom door, deep in thought and taking out her hairpins on the way.

Stopping dead in her tracks she drops a handful of pins on the landing, so they bounce from the polished floorboards and scatter in all directions.

No, Elspeth thinks as her face stretches first with realisation then with horror.

Please, no … No, no, no!

Chapter 25

1898—Clara

Clara barely hears the quiet tap on her bedroom door. Irritated at the interruption to her bedtime regime, she decides to ignore it and continue applying her cold cream. Then another tap comes but this time a little louder. They're not going to go away.

"Come in," she says, setting her little pot on the dressing table.

She turns in her chair still running her fingers around her face to see Garrison standing in the doorway. Who else would be knocking on my door at this time of night she thinks.

"May I come in?" he asks.

"Of course," she says politely.

Politeness and cordiality have become a way of life for them over the last two years. She doesn't recognise her husband as the force of nature he once was—humility has made him grow meek and mild. The Garrison of old was never known to be either of these things.

Sitting himself down in the small velvet chair by the fire he tightens his robe around his waist. He looks like a giant sitting on a thimble, uncomfortable and out of proportion, almost a ridiculous sight.

"Well, Clara," he says, "tonight has turned out to be quite an evening for so many reasons, don't you think?"

The question is rhetorical. He's shuffling in his seat, agitated whilst Clara sits perfectly still at the dressing table, hands clasped lightly in her lap. She was expecting this conversation after Garrison made the discovery that he and Annalise have mutual friends, but hoped he might have waited until morning.

"Indeed," she says with an air of indifference. It isn't her intention but the numbness she feels makes any response insincere or impossible. She knows exactly how this conversation will play out and lacks any sense of anticipation. Her eyes hold his until he looks away and clears his throat.

"Why didn't you tell me Annalise had become friendly with the Reid's? Surely you were concerned when you discovered as much yourself."

Concerned was an understatement. When Annalise gushed about her new-found friends Clara was preoccupied with thoughts about the decline of her marriage. It was all she could think about morning, noon and night; the situation with Hugo even taking a backseat. She forced herself to tune into conversations, but her mind was generally elsewhere.

Until Clara heard those names: Lilian, Elspeth— then her ears pricked. The ground shifted, she felt nauseous, but she nodded along as Annalise spoke, this time absorbing every single word of the conversation. And all the while Clara carefully studied every nuance her daughter displayed as she spoke.

For once Garrison might not even have existed.

"Of course, it has been disconcerting, but if I'm honest I thought the friendships might fizzle out naturally. Shamefully, I clung onto that hope for too long; how terrible that a mother should wish her daughter's friendships to end. Instead, they appear to be going from strength to strength. She's never really had female friends, not really, and now she has two. We should be happy for her."

Garrison takes a hold of his chin and closes his eyes, the words he wants to say are not coming easily. He takes a long breath.

"But they are her … mother and grandmother, surely the pain must be unbearable for you," he says.

How annoying he should feel the need to state the obvious. How unbelievably crass and insensitive. Some things are better left unsaid instead of being hammered home.

"Not quite unbearable, Garrison. I have managed to bear it as I have borne many things throughout our marriage," Clara snaps. "It's one of my few strengths," she adds sarcastically.

He jumps quickly to his feet, and she thinks he may storm out. How would I feel if he did this she wonders. Relieved he's out of her sight is the truthful answer. Even this sudden realisation doesn't upset her.

Instead, he strides to the window to look out into the darkness.

"Clara, we cannot go on like this. You must at least try to forgive me," he says with his back to her.

Once his sullen tone would have been like a stab to her heart and would have had her running to salve his wounds. She's all too aware now this only served to stroke his ego.

She has changed; he has changed her steadily over many a year, so even she didn't see it happening. Her pain, her anger, they have all fluttered away to indifference, the absolute opposite of love.

"I'm tired, I'd like to go to bed if you don't mind and resume our talk in the morning," she says.

Garrison strides towards her then drops to kneel at her feet. He buries his head in the cotton of her nightdress and prays she won't cast him aside. How he's missed the nearness of her, the smell of her. Her eyes stare at him day after day with a coldness he never thought he'd see. Never with Clara.

"Much has been happening over the last few months," she says now, pushing his hands away to get to her feet. She cannot bear his touch, his hot, damp breath on her thighs through her nightgown is repulsive.

She perches on the bed as Garrison stays on his knees, his hands hanging loosely between his legs feeling rejected and beaten. The wind howls down the chimney, but he remains silent, unsure how to bridge the distance between them.

If she's going to get him out of her room, she must speak some plain truths it seems.

"All these years I've tolerated your … indiscretions, looked the other way, because I convinced myself you couldn't help it. I even thought that you have so many temptations, so many women who desire you, how could you possibly resist forever? What a fool I've been. A man who is in love with his wife would respect her enough to keep temptation at arm's length knowing her heart would be broken if he should betray her trust."

He opens his mouth to speak but she holds up her hand.

"You went one step too far, Garrison, messing on your own doorstep as my grandfather would have said. I went to see Elspeth to find out the truth. I had to because the suspicion gnawed at me, until I was unable to function properly any longer. She was shocked of course to see me on her doorstep as I'm sure you can imagine. It was all so unlike me. Jarvis dropped me near to Bright Eye Lane in the carriage; I asked him to stop a few streets away as I fancied a walk to make a surprise visit to see you at Whitworth's. We agreed he would come back an hour later to collect me. I thought that was about the right amount of time to do what I needed to do. I was quite cunning about it. After checking I was alone, I snuck down the ginnel, you know, the one you will have snuck down so regularly. I did wonder if you might spot me from your window but decided it was the lesser of two evils by that point."

She can't lie, the look on his face is quite satisfying. Suddenly Clara no longer feels tired.

"Well, Elspeth was obviously keen to usher me inside and the feeling was mutual. I'd no intention of accepting her hospitality but then something quite unexpected happened. When I spoke with Elspeth, I found I liked her; in fact, really liked her. I saw what it is Annalise sees and no doubt what you did too: She is a beautiful woman, but she is a good woman."

Clara just had to say it aloud because she had to remind him what he was missing. She knew Elspeth was different to the others and she knew Garrison was in love with her. Clara could immediately see why, only minutes after stepping over her threshold. What surprised her the most was that the knowledge didn't make her feel jealous or resentful as she might have expected, it made her feel ... sad. Not for Garrison, but for herself and strangely for Elspeth. Of course, Elspeth was one half of the affair, but she was vulnerable, lonely and Garrison will have reacted to this in much the same way as he did with herself. She had been vulnerable and lonely when she met her husband.

In that moment Clara had clarity. Her husband was in love with two women at the same time in the same way. Sex is one thing; a simple act but love is quite another. It won't have taken long to fall in love with Elspeth, she thought; Garrison will have fallen in love with her almost instantly. She knows because in a strange way she felt love for this woman.

Of course, Clara will never be able to think of Elspeth as a friend, this would be a step too far. However, she will keep this fact to herself, it won't do Garrison any harm to think otherwise. It's useful for them to be on friendly terms for her daughter's sake.

"Oh, Clara," Garrison says now, his voice almost a whisper, "so much has happened without my knowledge. I live in another world and I'm no longer in the fold it seems."

Clara only nods. She doesn't need to tell him he took himself out of the fold by his actions.

"We've had many chats by the fireside since, Elspeth and me. How welcoming her home is, and in Stevie she has a man who adores her and has done all his life apparently. She wasn't sure at first about the relationship, but now she knows the only barrier to their love was age. But we all know age is no barrier at all, don't we? It's wonderful to see the glow she has about her when she talks of him."

"Stevie?" Garrison coughs out almost choking as he speaks.

The joy Clara feels in twisting the knife makes her lightheaded. She's long past feelings of jealousy, merely relishing the sense of justice she has.

"Of course, we had discussions about you, Garrison in the early days but to be fair, your name is barely mentioned nowadays and only by Annalise. Elspeth and I are however in agreement over one matter."

Garrison shakes his head gently, his eyes glassy.

"To what are you in agreement?" he asks, raising his head to look at her. He knows the answer won't be to his liking, but he has no option but to ask the question.

Clara stares intently into his eyes for a long second.

"Well, it was obvious to both of us really. Elspeth and I are convinced that you are Annalise's real father, that you concocted the adoption story like so many others. This was bad enough but then you had to seduce her grandmother," she looks down at her feet, "You disgust me."

The relief runs through Garrison like warm water. So, this is why his wife has rejected him all this time, for a misunderstanding which can so easily be rectified. Dropping his head back, he lets out a long breath which startles Clara.

"My love, I can't tell you how happy it makes me to tell you that you're very much mistaken, believe me. Stevie can vouch for me; it was he who came to ask for my help all those years ago. He will clarify the situation."

One short laugh escapes Clara.

"Garrison, Stevie and Elspeth are in love, deeply in love. Yes, I know he tried to take responsibility for being the father but he lied. To protect Lilian and spare the girl her mother's disapproval. So, I'm afraid Stevie's testimony to the truth is unreliable."

His mind is turning, turning; Clara and Elspeth believe him to have abused his position to seduce a teenage girl. How could they think so lowly of him? He stands determined to defend his last shred of honour.

"Clara, I assure you I am not Annalise's natural father. For heaven's sake, it seems you leave me with no alternative but to challenge Lilian. I must defend my reputation."

Jumping quickly from the bed, Clara plants her feet, hands on hips with a stance of defiance which startles her husband. What she lacks in height she makes up for with utter indignation, he thinks.

"You will do no such thing. I really don't care if you are Annalise's true father or not. This is only part of why I've grown so indifferent toward you, Garrison. You've made a complete and utter cuckold of me our entire married life and before for all I know. How I used to make excuses for you, how I felt I could never be enough for you. Why wouldn't you tire of a dull, mousy wife?"

"Clara, please, I love you, I've always loved you. I'm weak l know it but my love for you was never in question."

"Sadly, I know this to be true but it's not enough. I deserve better—I understand this now. I'm not mousy, I just prefer a quiet life. I'm not dull, I've just had to live in your shadow."

Walking to the door she turns to look at her husband.

"Annalise has grown fond of her new friends, even talking of them coming to London to hear her sing. Now, won't that be wonderful, darling?"

After staring at his wife for a moment, Garrison walks out slowly into the ice-cold corridor. He knows he will go mad if this turns out to be the case How could he watch on and see Elspeth with another man and Stevie of all people. Stevie … his boy.

Now his punishment is to watch on at Elspeth and Stevie's happiness. His chest tightens—what if Clara should fall in love with someone else too? He crumples to the floor, his back against the wall in more ways than one.

Clara hears her husband's distant snivelling as she climbs into bed, but she doesn't weep. She knows she's wept enough over Garrison Whitworth. Instead, she consoles herself that she should be grateful for what she has: a beautiful talented daughter, a grand home, money, status, stability. She has so much, and she can have all this forever if she wants it.

Nobody has it all, she knows this. Nobody.

She can have this life forever because neither she nor Garrison will risk the scandal of divorce for the sake of their daughter. He because it would break her heart to find out about her father's philandering ways and she because it might one day come to light with a little digging that Clara is the daughter of a murderer.

She and Garrison are bound as one forever; it is a small price to pay.

He's done his worst already, Clara thinks as she closes her eyes, so it can only get easier now.

Chapter 26

1898—Sissy

Elspeth reaches for Sissy's hand.

"Don't go, love," she says quietly, though her eyes are pleading, "I'm sure Annalise wouldn't mind you accompanying us in the carriage to Lilian's. She'd love to get to know you."

"Oh yes, your mama is quite right, it would be lovely if you could join us. I've heard so many nice things about you," Annalise says, her voice breathy, almost anxious, as though she wants to please her.

Surely, the girl can't be so keen for her to join them, and Sissy can't imagine the nice things her mother and Lilian have said. Sissy wasn't quick enough; she should have been on her way home by now.

She'd had a bellyful of her mother talking about Stevie and often wished she'd kept her mouth shut. It was a mistake. Now, he's asked her to marry him so there's no way she can move in now. Living with her mother and young stepfather at her age, how humiliating?

"Are you sure you need to be married?" Sissy asked her mother. The words were out before she could stop them.

"Congratulations, mam is really what you wanted to say, Sissy, isn't it?"

Her mother didn't say it unkindly, and Sissy mustered the customary response.

"Well, as you ask, I haven't needed to give it that much thought. Once I recovered from the shock and took things slowly, I realised I love him, he loves me so, what's to think about."

Oh, and Elspeth does love him. Garrison Whitworth rarely enters her mind and if he does it's fleeting. When she sees him at the factory, much like Clara she's discovered, she doesn't feel anything, not a thing. No hatred, no resentment, no sense of loss; this is how she knows their love couldn't have been real. At least not for her. Garrison is attractive, charismatic persistent, but above all, a man to fill the gaping chasm of loneliness. She isn't on the rebound, this is transparently clear to her now, the events in her life were simply in the wrong order. Had she discovered her love for Stevie first there would have been no need for a Garrison in her life.

Stevie only has to look at Elspeth and she finds herself smouldering his way, a hammering in her ears. She wants him badly, but he's a gentleman, and marriage is the only option for Stevie. If he doesn't marry her, he'll just be calling on her with a basket of wood and a kiss which leaves her wanting, forever. Elspeth is looking forward to being his wife, just the same as when she married before all those years ago. Frank would be delighted with her choice of man she often thinks. They both wanted the other to find happiness again should they be left alone.

For so long Elspeth longed to tell Stevie she had fallen in love with him, but the timing had to be perfect.

When will that be she often asked herself, but she knew she shouldn't force it to happen. In the end, as with many things in her life, the timing was unimportant, only living the moment made it perfect.

Stevie was stoking the fire one Saturday night when he turned his head to see her watching him, her intense expression unsettling. Poker in hand, he felt a compulsion to get to his feet and proclaim, "I love you, Elspeth."

The blood hurtling around her head made his voice seem far away. Stevie was not a man for proclamations.

"And I love you, my darling man," she said instantly.

Their eyes filled and he knelt at her feet and kissed her gently, poker still in hand as if he'd forgotten it was there. It was so simple yet so profound. A pivotal moment in her life yet it was as though they said those words all the time. Stevie's love is as sure as the sky above; always there without question, always will be.

Elspeth looks at Sissy staring out of her kitchen window now. She will be able to see very little through the nets, but it will be preferable to looking at Annalise's earnest expression.

Did I subconsciously want to meet the girl Sissy wonders; she knows she could have left at any point this afternoon.

"Will you come?" Annalise asks.

Sissy has nowhere to turn, nowhere to run. Usually this would make her bare her teeth, but today is different. Today she submits.

"Yes … thank you, that will be very pleasant.

How she is going to get through the next few hours she has no idea. Lily seems to cope she thinks, but then lying has become second nature to my sister.

As the cobbled streets of Bright Eye Lane disappear from view, Annalise enquires where Sissy lives.

Bracing herself, Sissy knows this is only the first of many questions.

"I live with my husband Samuel near the pithead. It's just a few streets away from mam ... my mother. He was a miner before he retired. Mam ... my mother probably told you my sons are grown and left home.

"I always think mum and mam sound so much more affectionate than mother or mama," Annalise says, smiling, "Do your sons works at the colliery?"

Sissy is mesmerised by the bow of Annalise's lips and the golden hue of her cheeks. She is a beautiful girl with the same dark hair and colouring as the rest of the family, Sissy thinks, looking away quickly when she realises that she's staring.

"Sorry, I'm asking too many questions, aren't I? You must feel like your under interrogation," Annalise says.

"No, not at all. I'm still getting used to the boys living away from home is all," Sissy lies, "Yes, they're both miners like their father. Not much else for them around here except Whitworth's but Sam said they should follow in their father's footsteps."

Elspeth glances at Sissy and smiles encouragingly. See, this is nice isn't it, Sissy can almost hear her mother thinking.

"I've come to look forward to our little jaunts to Lilian's," Elspeth says, "I do enjoy our little chats."

"As do I," Annalise says brightly.

She seems so young in some ways and an old soul in others, Sissy thinks as the carriage comes to a stop outside Lilian's cottage. She's a contradiction.

Burton helps them down in turn and Elspeth leads the way up the path and through the front door.

"Only us, Lilian," she says, "We have a surprise for you today."

Lilian turns from the range and tries to hide her look of disappointment with a false smile as she welcomes her guests. Nobody notices but Sissy as they take off their coats and hang them on the peg by the front door. There are no airs and graces here apparently, Sissy notices, they're all very cosy with one another.

She tries to shake the festering resentment which follows her around like a dog at her heels.

Lilian ladles soup into bowls and cuts bread fresh from the oven. Quite the little housewife, Lily, Annalise will be impressed, Sissy thinks as she tries to swallow down her irritability along with her soup.

There's a slight tremor to her hand as she raises her spoon. Lilian notices and looks away quickly but not before Sissy spots her sister's scrutiny. She's taken to having the odd glass of gin after Samuel goes to the pub of an evening and she can't see there's anything wrong with it. Sitting down with her crochet and a little tipple has become something to look forward to; it gets her through the days. One glass can sometimes lead to another and perhaps more of late, but from tonight she thinks she might start cutting down.

She listens to her mother and Annalise chatting, blissfully unaware of the awkward interaction going on right under their noses.

Sissy's bread is sticking in her craw. She shouldn't have come she knows now, fighting the urge to down her spoon and walk out the front door. Annalise's voice cuts into her distress.

"Your mama and Lilian may have said, but my husband Hugo has been quite unwell these last two years. An apoplexy I'm afraid. Thankfully, he seems to be on the mend, and I hope to return to singing very soon," she says.

Sissy feels a clamminess under her dress as they all turn to look her way.

"I'm pleased to hear your husband has made a recovery," Sissy says politely. She takes the empty bowls to the sink for something to do.

"Thank you, you're very kind. I've invited your mama and Lilian to come to London as my guest and they have agreed. It would mean a great deal to me if you wanted to accompany them."

Dropping the bowls in the sink, one bowl now swims around the soapy water in pieces. Sissy forefinger is cut but she runs it under the tap and wraps the tea towel around it. How she'd hate to draw attention to her trembling hands at present.

"That's a very nice offer, but I'm not sure if I could spare the time away from home," Sissy says, "My husband can't seem to cope without me."

The last thing on earth she wants is to spend an entire weekend on a tense excursion with her mother and sister.

Annalise chuckles pleasantly saying, "Hugo would be the same without staff, he hasn't a clue about housekeeping. Well, you and your husband would be very welcome if you decided to join them."

Join them? Join them! She's been made an outcast in this little clan, Sissy thinks.

"Oh, you've cut your finger," Annalise says her voice high-pitched with concern.

Sissy looks down to see blood seeping through the tea towel.

Elspeth rushes to help but Sissy snatches her hand away in panic.

"I'm perfectly alright mam, but perhaps it might be time I was on my way. I'm sorry to be a bother."

Lilian fires a look at her sister. They've barely been together two minutes and now she's cutting the gathering short. She wouldn't put it past Sissy to have done it deliberately. How rude she is, always thinking about herself and nobody else.

Sissy forces herself to join in the polite conversation on the way home as best she can until the carriage drops her well away from home. She makes sure of it as the last thing she needs is having to explain herself to Samuel when he hears the gossip.

With a fixed smile she waves to her mother and Annalise until they disappear into the twilight. Sissy can't deny how lovely Annalise is and she has a sudden pang which springs tears to her eyes. To think the last time that she cried was the morning after dada's funeral when she decided crying wasn't going to help her mother. She remembers how strong she was then; how her mother and Lilian leaned on her.

As Sissy opens the front door, Edna and Doreen from the street stop their nattering to give her a wave. She's never been one to stand on street wittering on about the price of fish, but perhaps she should have done more of it, so she wouldn't feel such an outcast.

What a day she thinks getting a clean rag from the drawer for her finger. As if I don't have enough on my plate, what with my nasty husband, my mother like a lovesick schoolgirl, and my sister lying merrily through her back teeth.

Checking the mantle clock and knowing Samuel will be back from the afternoon session at the pub soon she wraps her finger quickly. She must get his tea on.

She can't help her mind wandering to Annalise. That girl seems almost too good to be true which means she probably is. She can hear her mother's voice in her head saying, "Now, Sissy if you look for the faults you will surely find them."

But try as she might, Sissy can't deny she's fallen under the spell of Ms Annalise Paterson, much like the rest of the family.

Her eyes go to the cupboard where she's hidden the gin bottle behind her crochet bag. Perhaps tonight isn't the night to stop having a little snifter after all.

Tomorrow will be better.

Chapter 27

1898—Annalise

"You've had her to yourself long enough, Hugo my dear friend, it's time to unlock the door and release the princess from the tower."

Howie takes a long drag on his cigar then shares a chuckle with Hugo.

"She won't leave me, though I've tried my best to boot her back to London many a time," Hugo says.

I look between the two partners in crime.

"Ahem, I am here you know, gentlemen."

Hugo looks dashing in his evening suit, his hair freshly cut, his face freshly shaven. To look at him you'd be forgiven for thinking the events of the last two years had never happened; if it wasn't for the fact he tires easily and can't walk very far one would be hoodwinked. The tremors have long since ceased though his grip remains weak. To me, his recovery is nothing short of a miracle, but he remains quietly frustrated. A firm handshake is the mark of a man, he says, mourning its loss.

"Papa is waiting for his private audience, Annalise, he has been very patient and understanding," Howie says.

"He has indeed, and I shan't keep him waiting much longer."

Where are the butterflies I used to feel at the thought of singing? They elude me, now being replaced by a small drop of my stomach. I'm enjoying being at home too much, especially now I've made such true friends. Elizabeth Gilbert is a kind and considerate companion, but true female friends of any kind have eluded me throughout my life.

"Can I ask you something, Howie?"

"Oh dear, this sounds serious."

"Well, I've just been wondering if retiring at my peak would be the best option."

Howie's head darts in my direction as he sits forward in his seat.

"Why would you say such a thing; you're hardly old or past your best. Are you thinking of retiring?"

"In theory I could. We certainly don't need any more money," I say.

He looks at me astounded, his mouth opening and closing. He no doubt wants to find the perfect response for maximum impact. It would surprise him to know I've thought of every response he might deliver.

"Annalise, if you retired now then the world will be deprived of their little songbird far too soon."

"You're very sweet," I concede, smiling his way.

"But I don't think the world would appreciate me forcing them to listen to a fading voice either, Howie. Sometimes one must recognise that one's priorities in life change, not only through need or circumstance but because we change within."

"In my view, you should wait until you're back in the saddle before making a decision," Hugo chips in, "I think you may simply have nothing more than a dose of the collywobbles after so long away from the limelight. I've heard you singing, and your voice is as remarkable as ever."

I take a sip of port. I've been weighing up the options for so long I'm thinking in circles. My concern is less about my voice and more about returning to my old lifestyle. I finally feel I belong, not on a professional level but on a personal one. I recognise now that I've been running around desperate to get home, not a physical home but a spiritual one. Life as a child at Hardcastle was too lonely to feel like home.

But now is not the time to articulate my feelings and if in doubt, do nowt as papa says, coining a phrase he once heard his own papa use.

"Perhaps, you're right, Hugo," I say, "I didn't enjoy being at home to begin with but then when you became better and I had my visits to Haigh, I found balance," I turn to Howie, "Never fear, your papa will have his private audience come what may."

Getting to my feet the men join me and I kiss the cheek of my husband and then my dear friend before I make my way upstairs. Placing the candle on the nightstand I see Minnie has my night things laid out on the bed and the bed warmer in position. She used to help me undress for bed but after Hugo was ill, I became more independent. The staff had enough to do without fussing around me when I could manage perfectly well on my own for the most part. Nowadays, I prefer the privacy and solitude of my bedroom.

I've been devouring my latest book, *The Turn of the Screw.* Reading is another new-found pleasure and I settle back on the pillows with a sigh. This is the peace of mind I think about often, the sheer pleasure of a good night's sleep ahead with a clear mind. Whereas the day ahead used to loom when Hugo was ill, now I have so much to look forward to.

I have Elspeth to thank for this book, she enjoys reading, often passing on recommendations. How easy I find her company and Lilian too. I haven't seen Sissy since the day she cut her finger, but Elspeth says Samuel keeps her busy and she's a bit of a loner, preferring her own company.

"There you are, waiting up like a good little wife," Hugo teases, sitting on the edge of the bed. Taking off his shoes he lies back and turns his head to look at me.

"You know, you grow more beautiful each passing year," he says, reaching to touch a lock of my hair.

"Oh you, that's the brandy talking," I say, though I admit I love how he admires me so, "Are you wanting some attention my love per chance."

I laugh but he doesn't join in, instead he gets to his knees and takes my face between his palms.

"I mean it," he says, "Lord knows how I would have made it through without you, my darling, you have gone above and beyond the duties of any wife. I'm so lucky to have you, I think if I didn't, I might not have … have made it. I know I kept going because of you."

His lips touch mine gently and I feel the depth of love for a while until the tender kiss builds to a fervour. His tongue finds its way into my mouth. My body responds, my nipples hardening under the cotton of my bodice, so he reaches to run his fingers over them. His lips trail lower and lower until he lifts my nightdress to stroke between my thighs and I moan my pleasure. I watch as he quickly discards his clothes and then I pull my nightdress over my head. He stands and stares at me, his eyes devouring me until he must use his hands to take what he wants, what he needs. Sliding his way into me he holds my buttocks firmly, so I feel the intensity of him. As his grinding mounts so does my groaning and he joins me. I forget myself for a while as does Hugo. We even forget ourselves at the crucial moment leaving Hugo shuddering and panting into my hair.

"I'm sorry," he says after a moment when he returns to me, "I don't know what happened to us. I lost myself in you like never before, I couldn't help myself. You should have stopped me."

I rise onto my elbow to look at his dear face, the face I thought might leave me forever to lie alone in the unending darkness not so long ago.

"I didn't want you to stop, I'm not sorry because it was beautiful, our lovemaking always is," I say, "We've been playing with fire for a long time and what will be will be. I'm restless, Hugo. Perhaps I'm ready to start a new phase of life if … if you are."

As his hand cups my cheek I nuzzle into the gentleness of his touch and see the wetness of his eyes.

"My darling girl, I've been ready since the day I met you.

You only ever had to say the word."

Chapter 28

1898—Annalise

"Sissy, what the hell are you doing," Elspeth screams from the station gate.

We all turn in unison to see her running down the platform, skirts in hand, dark hair falling further from her bun with each step.

My hand drops from my mouth as Donald jumps from the train; he's just this minute pulled to a stop. Mama is crying softly, and I'm sure I would be crying too if I could only begin to process the chaos before me.

My eyes dart to Lilian to see she's perilously close to the blade of Sissy's paring knife. Sissy's knuckles are as white as her face and it's clear to all of us she will not be letting go, even with the sudden appearance of her mother. She looks completely crazed at this moment.

Donald holds up his hand and Elspeth stops in her tracks, blowing out air in great clouds. Smoke from the train gives the whole scene an unreal atmosphere.

"Now, I think we all need to calm down or somebody's going to get hurt, accidentally or … otherwise," he says in his familiar broad Yorkshire accent.

His train driver's cap is pulled well down over his eyes to cover his face but there's no mistaking the terror in his voice.

"Sissy, be reasonable, come inside so we can have a cup of tea and a chat. There's no need for all this, love," Elspeth says quietly, her voice breaking.

Sissy's desperate eyes fly between us all. I feel sick. She's gone to another place, I think, I can't imagine she's open to reason even from her mother.

"I've had a bellyful of tea and sympathy; I'm drowning in it. I don't want to talk, I want Lily to tell the truth for once," Sissy says, spittle glistening on her chin like frost.

"Please, Sissy, listen to what your mother is saying, this is neither the time nor the place," mama says wiping her eyes with her handkerchief.

Lilian's wide eyes are fixed on the blade next to her breast. She isn't crying though her lips are trembling.

"Will you tell the truth; can you even tell it?" Sissy asks Lilian in a low voice that I struggle to hear.

Her eyes travel up to meet her sisters.

"Do you want me to tell the truth, Sissy? Do you … really?"

Eyes locked, the sisters' expressions are pure hatred. I don't understand why they would hate each other so. Nothing is making sense.

I feel a waft of air as Donald takes the opportunity to lunge forward and grab Sissy by the shoulders. She stumbles backwards flailing and swearing. Elspeth rushes to pull the knife from her daughter's hand but Sissy has tight hold. I watch them flailing wildly, terrified that one of them will be slashed or worse in the fracas.

"Stop!" I hear myself shouting, "For god's sake stop it before one of you gets killed!"

I rush forward with mama on my heels when Sissy turns, and the blade finds its way through my sleeve and down the top of my arm. I hear mama screaming before Sissy's face distorts with a look of horror and she drops to her knees sobbing, the knife falling to the ground. In a flash, Elspeth recovers the blade and throws it into the bushes over the train track.

As I watch it fly through the air the world seems to stop just for the merest flicker and then it gathers speed. Everyone runs past Sissy to my side including Donald.

"I'm fine, I'm fine," I say quickly, though I'm not sure if I am. I wince as Donald takes my arm from my coat to take a good look but there's hardly any blood to be seen on my dress. My coat saved me from any drastic injury.

He whirls round, his face puce shouting, "What in god's name got into you, woman, you could have killed her? I'll go and fetch Constable Hardisty."

"I'm sorry, I'm so sorry," Sissy sobs over and over rocking on her knees on the station platform.

Mama steps forward to put a hand on Donald's shoulder.

"There's no need for the police to be summoned, Donald," she says quietly, looking at Elspeth and Lilian, "Is there?"

The women shake their heads before looking at the ground.

"Thank you for intervening, Donald. I will be eternally indebted to you, and I mean to recompense you for your bravery, believe me. But now I think we all need that cup of tea."

Donald's brow creases as he drops his hand from my arm.

"I don't want any money, Mrs Harper if that's what you're on about but I still think you should take this further. She's mad, she is," he says pointing to Sissy, "she's not fit to be out."

Elspeth reaches down to pull Sissy to her feet, but Sissy can't meet her mother's eyes. Instead, she leans against Elspeth snivelling and visibly quaking under the lamplight.

Nobody speaks for what seems an age, we can only stare at the miserable sight.

Donald startles us when he breaks the silence.

"Well, I'll say no more about it then if you've made up your mind," Donald says, addressing me, "but make sure you get that arm looked at."

"I will, Donald," I say touching his arm to try and calm him.

"Right, well, I'll bid you all a goodnight then. Best get Bessie back to the shed," he says, referring to his beloved engine.

Lifting his cap, he walks down the station and turns to look at me before he climbs aboard. We're all silent until eventually the steam billows and weaves around us before chasing the train down the track.

I have a sudden urge to board the train but it's too late, I must stay and face my fate. But I'm certain it won't be a tale I want to hear tonight.

Or indeed ever.

*

I know it should be me who leads the way to return to the manor but taking the first step seems impossible.

Mama takes my hand, and her gentle touch makes tears burn the back of my eyes. I take gulp after gulp of night air as though I'm drowning.

Lilian and Elspeth, arms wrapped around Sissy, follow us in a dishevelled procession down the pathway. We must look a fright.

I'm so glad to see Sutcliffe when he appears in the hallway not long after our arrival. He's the epitome of professionalism, though I'm sure he must be taken aback by my sudden reappearance with three strange women and mama. He relieves us of our coats and gloves. I doubt he will remember Lilian as the woman who landed on our doorstep two years ago. His level tone is soothing as he comments on the cold, damp weather and I cling to the familiarity.

I try not to wince as my sleeve travels down my wounded arm, thankful for the dark colour of my dress to hide the small bloodstain. Rubbing my trembling hands together I'm struggling to remember the niceties of receiving guests.

Hugo appears from the sitting room, paper in hand.

"What the …" he says, his expression agog before remembering his manners, "Sorry, I thought you would be well on your way to London by now, Annalise."

Then follows a general 'How do you do?' to everyone else.

Inclining his head in the direction of mama then everyone else in turn he stands looking my way. I come to my senses, finally realising the ball is in my court.

"Darling, there's been a change of plan. These are my friends the Reid's whom you've heard so much about. They need my help with something urgent this evening. I wonder if you might leave us to chat in the parlour. I'll be in to see you shortly."

He doesn't want to leave me I know as he can see I'm upset but I raise my eyebrows almost pleading for his compliance. I'm relieved when he eventually backs away from us down the hallway, saying, "Of course, I shall see you all soon then, after your little … chat."

Closing his study door as slowly as possible his eyes rest upon me and I manage to muster a smile. It will bring him little comfort, but it must suffice for the time being.

I ask Sutcliffe to bring refreshments before I lead the way into the parlour. The fire is roaring away, and I see the indent in the cushion and the paraphernalia Hugo left behind: a discarded cigar, an empty cup and saucer, a half-eaten shortbread, quickly moving them to the windowsill out of sight. How strange I should feel the need to bother under the circumstances.

"Please, take a seat," I say pointing to the chaise longue. Elspeth and her daughters look at one another before sitting in a line. Elspeth positions herself in the middle, still wanting to keep the sisters apart subconsciously or otherwise.

I wonder if I look as unkempt as everyone else. I'm quite sure I must do.

"I'd like to take a look at your injury first if I may, Annalise," mama says.

Holding out my arm I reassure her it's merely a scratch. The last thing I want is mama fussing as I'm desperate now to get to the root of this evening's dramatic events. My arm is the least of my worries at present.

"You can see it before you leave, mama, I promise," I tell her with a weak smile.

She looks away unable to meet my eyes I sense, and I haven't a clue what to say. The gathered party is waiting for my next move but where to begin.

Elspeth finally breaks the silence with a sigh.

"Look, the time has come for the truth, Clara, girls," she says turning her head left and right to address mama and her daughters simultaneously, "There is no other way. Enough is enough don't you think."

My jaw is so tight it's paining me as I look between them. I'm clearly missing something here but its apparent they all know what it is. They are all bound by a secret.

"Yes, I would be very grateful if you could tell me what tonight was all about," I say, "In truth, I think I deserve an explanation."

My tone leaves the women in no doubt about how my patience is running dry.

Mama clears her throat, and I look her way.

"I think it only right that I should be the one to explain, my dear," she says, "This is very difficult for all of us, but … but I'm afraid you must prepare yourself for a shock."

I tilt my chin and stare at my mother. She still cannot meet my eyes, instead she scrabbles for a handkerchief in her bag, holding it tightly in her hand but not crying.

"I'm afraid I must tell you that I … I … I …"

She can't continue it seems but I'm getting past myself.

"Please go on, you are what, mama?"

The words fire out of my mouth more harshly than I have ever spoken to her before.

"I am not your real mother."

A strange laugh escapes me and seems to reverberate in the air between us. I must have misheard surely.

I'm startled by a sharp rap on the door and Sutcliffe, with immaculate timing, if unintended on this occasion, appears with a tea tray. As he expertly pours the tea, I study the faces of the women sitting in my parlour. They're somehow steadily changing from being the familiar friendly faces I've come to care so much about, blurring to slowly become the faces of strangers—every single one of them.

"Will that be all, madam?" Sutcliffe asks.

"Yes, thank you, Sutcliffe," I say out of habit.

Once the heavy door has closed my eyes rest upon the person I think of as my mother. She looks old and tired suddenly.

Mama is still talking but her words have stopped registering. They have all been playing a part, a role and it seems nothing has been real my whole life. I'm too taken aback to cry even. Sitting amidst mama's babble of words I try to piece together my own scattered thoughts.

After a while I ask flatly: "So, who is my real mother?"

But before anyone can answer I'm already one step ahead. My gaze fixes on Elspeth.

"Are my real mother?" I finally ask.

Shaking her head, Elspeth's lip are set in a thin line.

"No, my dear, it isn't me, I'm not your mother," she almost whispers.

She doesn't elaborate. I look at Lilian and Sissy sitting beside their mother.

"Then who is?" I ask curtly, tired of the gameplaying.

I hear mama sigh as she drops her head back and closes her eyes.

"Lilian is your real mother, Annalise. Your father and I adopted you. Lilian was just a young girl," she says.

She takes a breath to go on, but I hold up my hand, so she clamps her mouth shut and waits.

"I'm sorry, I don't want to hear any more right now."

This is all too much. I'd like to run and fetch Hugo, but I know this is a conversation for us women and us alone. Instead, I walk to the window to put some distance between us. The fog in the garden hangs low and I imagine myself walking out into the swirl of it and disappearing.

"Annalise, please, if you hear me or not, you must know that your father and I longed for a child for many years, and you were sent to us as a gift from heaven. Adopting you is the best thing I ever did in my life. I only regret not telling you, but this wasn't done with malice, it was to protect you."

Sissy startles us with a deep and sinister laugh before jumping to her feet. I'm alarmed—the woman is clearly unhinged and out of control.

"How can you just sit there, Lilian? she says. "Now is the time to stop the lying once and for all."

Lilian doesn't respond. She only remains seated, staring at her sister with a deadpan expression.

"Look, if you don't tell her then I will," Sissy says.

Lilian remains impassive as we wait. Eventually she gets to her feet and calmly invites her sister to sit down. Although Sissy's face is flushed with anger, she does as she's told for once and re-joins her mother on the chaise.

Mama remains perfectly still, her eyes narrowing like a suspicious cat contemplating its prey.

They all seem so near yet so far away.

As I sit, another question suddenly appears.

"So, if you are my mother, Lilian, then who pray tell is my father?"

The answer will have to wait. I run without thinking to mama when I hear a noise escaping her which can only be described as that of a wounded animal.

The terrible sound will surely live with me the rest of my days.

Chapter 29

1902 – The Whitworths

Hugo appears at the breakfast table bleary-eyed. Florence wouldn't settle after a nightmare but once he'd soothed her, he decided to write. Annalise purses her lips in mock reprimand at the sight of him. His eyes are craggy, highlighting his tiredness. She still can't help worrying he might have a relapse though the worry has lessened over the years.

"I know, I know, I should leave it to Butterfield but I was awake anyway and then I thought I might as well tidy my jumbled thoughts. I hate to lie awake with them in a knot."

Annalise smiles. It's a weak excuse. He just wants to spend time with his darling daughter and she doesn't mind one little bit. Family is everything and should be kept close, not at arms' length, she believes. Engaging a nanny was merely conforming to old standards when in truth they would both be more than happy to incorporate more modern ways into their marriage if they dared to.

"Good morning, papa," Florence says sweetly, reaching out both hands to her father. He swoops to picks her up and sit on his knee at the table, asking what her nightmare was about.

Shaking her head, Annalise doesn't want to point out yet again he should leave her to sit in her seat at the table now she's almost four or she will grow spoilt.

She doesn't bother saying it as she knows their daughter could never be spoilt by love because she herself had everything, including doting parents and was far from spoilt. Soon enough Florence shan't want to sit on her papa's knee.

"Did you know that mama is going to teach me to play the piano, papa?" Florence says her violet eyes round and sparkling. She plays with his beard, and he pulls a face to make her laugh.

Annalise knows her life may seem idyllic, but no life is without its trials. She's learnt this now.

"She is? Well, you will have a very good teacher. Did you know your mother was—or should I say is—a very famous opera singer?" he says.

Florence looks unimpressed: "I think I'd like to be a famous piano player. Can we start today, mama?"

"We'll see, darling, perhaps before tea. Mama may have other things to do today," she tells her.

Hugo looks at the letter his wife was reading now folded neatly on the table in front of her.

"News?" he asks buttering his toast with one hand.

She doesn't answer, only pulls the cord to summon Miss Butterfield, who quickly appears after knocking. She's a prim but kindly woman whom Annalise instantly took a liking to. It wasn't a difficult decision as the other nannies were too austere and she prefers a more moderated approach to raising children.

"Yes, madam," she says, and Annalise thinks how she's never seen her anything other than measured and calm even when Florence was a trying toddler. She has greying, curly hair which springs loose at the side of her ear throughout the day no matter how hard to tries to plaster it to her head. Annalise finds this charming though she knows if she told her she would be self-conscious.

"I may need to go out later, Miss Butterfield, I'm not sure yet. Can you take Florence a little early this morning please so I can have a chat with Mr Hugo?"

"Certainly, madam," she says, "Come Florence, let us put on our coats to go outside. It's such a beautiful morning."

Florence leaves the room holding her nanny's hand. By the time the door closes they've already decided Florence will wear her green coat to match her dress today.

"Oh, dear, I don't know why but I feel I must prepare myself for a ticking off," Hugo says as soon as they're alone.

"No, nothing like that," Annalise laughs, "I've just had a little shock this morning."

"I see. The note?" he asks, his expression quizzical.

Nodding, she hands him the letter. They stare at each other a second or two until he starts to read, and she watches his face intently for clues.

Dear Annalise,

I'm still not sure if I'm doing the right thing in contacting you after so long but I felt I must write and ask the question.

Please would you visit my home on Bright Eye Lane at your earliest convenience so we might have a discussion?

The offer is made in good faith, and I hope you will accept as there are some things I would like to explain.

However, if you feel this is not possible, I will of course understand, and I will never contact you again.

Yours,
Elspeth

Hugo folds the note carefully again and places it back on the table.

"Well, this is a turn up," he says, quietly, "What will you do?"

Annalise stares out of the glass doors and spots the little wooden gate to the station which has long since seen an arrival or departure.

"Whatever I do, I think I must do it today or not at all. This cannot hang over me any longer," she says.

Hugo pulls her gently to her feet with both hands. She leans into his chest and breathes his clean smell as his arms loosely circle her waist.

"I think you may have already answered my question; if the situation hangs over you then what will be different tomorrow without an answer or an explanation?"

Raising her head, she swims in the eyes of her husband. If she didn't know before, she knows without doubt she made the right decision all those years ago to leave the glamour of London behind.

*

As the carriage approaches Hardcastle House, Annalise studies her childhood home, her mind replaying episodes from her time spent growing up here. She took the beauty of it for granted as she's sure Florence will also do with her home as she grows. Perhaps it is the same way for all children; for good or ill, their childhood, is all they know.

Clara is waiting for her in the sitting room, her silver hair coiffed into an elegant chignon at the nape of her neck. Annalise quickly wonders if she may have been expecting her visit.

"Darling, how lovely to see you," she says, returning her daughter's peck on her cheek.

"You look pretty today, mama," she says sitting in the chair opposite her mother like the old days.

They take tea but Annalise is quiet; contemplating how to start the conversation. Whichever way she turns she knows she will be opening old wounds which have yet to heal properly. Will they ever heal she wonders.

"So, my dear, I think the time has come to stop walking on eggshells. I'm aware it's no coincidence you are here; I assume you have received a note from Elspeth this morning."

Annalise's eyes widen and her mouth forms a distinct 'o' shape, so Clara can't help but smile before going on.

"So much time has passed, time where I've felt as though I've lost my daughter though she's been right in front of me. I know most of the story but I'm still missing some of the pieces and I for one would love to hear an explanation. It seems you are of the same mind."

Placing her cup on the tray Annalise leans back in her seat, lowering her eyes. She's flustered under her mother's gaze and somehow feels she must quickly catch up with her.

"You are suddenly being very candid, mama, I'm not sure what to make of it after so long."

Clara smiles ruefully at her daughter.

"Make of it what you will, I'm weary of trying to turn a blind eye to the elephant in the room. I'm exhausted by it even."

Annalise lets out a sigh, suddenly realising she was holding her breath. She's so unused to honest and open conversation with her mother nowadays.

"Dear me, this is not what I expected this morning. I thought I might have to convince you I should speak to Elspeth. I'm taken aback though I can't tell you how relieved I am to discover we're united in how we feel."

Annalise looks warmly into her mother's eyes, her awkwardness ebbing away a little. It feels pleasant.

"Understandably, you were so distressed that night and then time passes and somehow, we've never spoken of it since. I sensed however we both wanted to on many occasions. I've been avoiding you it's true, and you and papa haven't been as involved in Florence's life as we would have liked. I only didn't want to hurt your feelings or make you think anything had changed," she pauses, "But like it or not, everything has changed. The only thing that hasn't is how much I love you."

The women's eyes mist and its now Clara's turn to hold her breath.

"I'm sorry, mama, I've been so upset, not just with you, but with everyone. I didn't feel ready to talk about it. Now though I'd like to know more, I'm ready to know more. I'm so relieved we're singing from the same song sheet."

Garrison suddenly appears in the doorway, startling the women who are so engrossed in their conversation.

"Is it safe to come in?" he asks sheepishly.

Laughing, Annalise and Clara beckon him into the room. Annalise notices how drawn and older he looks these days, and the guilt rises in her.

Clara asked him to give them some time alone before he joined them. He'd rather not know what Elspeth has up her sleeve, but Clara is keen for a clean slate, a fresh start for all of them. Why rake over old coals when no good can come of it he wonders but Clara is insistent. Perhaps he's only thinking of his own needs.

"Annalise and I will be heading off shortly, Garrison. I'm not sure how long we will be, so have dinner without me if I'm back late," Clara tells her husband.

This new version of my wife has slowly been revealing itself, Garrison thinks. It took him a while to realise but she's franker and more assertive nowadays around him. His timid little wife has gone, though this is hardly surprising.

He's grateful to Clara and Elspeth for not enlightening Annalise about his failings. Clara could have disclosed his part in the situation at any time, he's well aware of it and the thought has been a constant noose around his neck. Perhaps she's protecting their daughter rather than him but either way he's thankful for small mercies.

"How are you, my dear?" Garrison asks his daughter, trying one last ditch attempt, "As I told you before, it's never too late to change course."

Clara shoots him a peevish look and he immediately regrets his words.

Annalise thinks of the advice her father gave her when she was poised to take London by storm. Heading across the room to face him, she kisses his cheek.

"I think I'm strong enough now to face the situation head on, papa. But know this before we go: you and mama have been fine parents. I needed some time to pass, even to become a parent myself to have such clarity. Whatever happens this afternoon, you and mama will not be replaced, not today … not ever."

Garrison hangs his head. Though he's touched by her words the pride he feels sours quickly to shame. A shame that will surely follow him around forever he thinks.

Clara joins them, lightly touching her husband's bowed head. When he raises it to look at her, his eyes are glistening her way. For the first time in years, something he feels affects her.

"Annalise is quite right, Garrison, you have been a fine father," she says.

He bites down hard on his lip to control himself. His wife's endorsement cuts him to the quick. He may have been a fine father, but he has been a terrible husband is the hidden meaning behind her words.

Is it too late for them he wonders. Perhaps, but then he must continue to prove his loyalty to her. Five years have passed, and he hasn't looked at another woman and he's no intention of straying again. He's learned what he had and lost the hard way, but he worries Clara will forever remain unconvinced. Lack of hope is harder to live with some days more than others. Some mornings he wakes and forgets she's not by his side. The disappointment when he reaches for her in bed and she's not there is devastating. He often weeps but then becomes annoyed with himself as self-pity is an unseemly trait. All he can do is get up to face another day. Perhaps he may see more of his daughter and granddaughter if this afternoon goes well, and they could be his focus.

He tries not to think of the day Elspeth married Stevie. It was a trial, and he found the complexity of his emotions overwhelming. Under normal circumstances they would have been invited as Stevie's guest but instead Clara retreated to her room for the weekend feigning illness, whilst Garrison laced his wounds with brandy.

Stevie's worthy of her which is harder to swallow. He was a fine boy who became a good man.

He knows the two of them are made for each other, and this too sits uneasily with Garrison. For a time, he tortured himself by staring down into their little kitchen from his office, watching them living their life together. They are loving and affectionate and the expressions on their faces became his penance.

Now his desk has been moved to the other side of the room. It was for the best.

Stevie waited quietly in the wings until his hand was forced, he discovered. Elspeth looks up to him as do her daughters and though it's hard for Garrison to admit, they were meant to be a family.

Garrison was lucky enough to have his own family to cherish but he was always looking over his shoulder for the next opportunity. How strange Stevie should be the one to highlight the error of his ways. Now the apprentice is teaching the master.

Part of him will always love Elspeth, he knows it, but he never for one moment stopped loving his wife and he could never have left her, with or without Annalise. His love only grows stronger and perhaps this will be enough to save them. Time will tell. His daughter is quite right, he thinks, sometimes time is the only ingredient needed.

Some things simply cannot be rushed.

Chapter 30

1902—Annalise

The plan is set.

Burton hand delivered a message to Elspeth confirming we would like to pay her a visit this very afternoon if this would be convenient. He returned promptly with a note saying she was looking forward to receiving us.

Bright Eye Lane is as immaculate as always when we arrive. Papa has maintained the traditions of my grandpapa, to ensure the lane is still the most coveted place to live in the town. Children are playing out as it's a Saturday and some stand and watch the carriage as it drives past like they used to when I visited before. Often the children would stroke the horses when they came to a standstill, and they do the same today. As Burton helps us dismount, I listen to the children asking questions about the horses.

It's as though we called yesterday, as though nothing has happened in the between years.

Apprehension flutters within me, but I remind myself I'm the one in charge of this conversation. I know there's nothing to fear from this encounter though it looms large; nerves must not get the better of me this afternoon. Nerves will be the barrier to the truth.

I wonder how long Burton will have to wait as I open the back gate of number two. I must stay and face the music however uncomfortable the meeting may become. This is not a day to run away before I have found out all the answers to my questions. This day must start a brand-new chapter.

Even before I place my foot on the first of the stone steps to the door, Elspeth appears, her smile hesitant. I'm unsure whether to return it for a second or two. Finally, my lips curve slightly of their own accord, and Elspeth's smile widens in response.

She's only slightly aged in the last five years, her hair still showing barely a smattering of grey. She's wearing what I imagine is her best dress of dark blue with a white lace collar. How beautiful she looks smiling through her strained expression.

"I'm so happy to see you both," she says, "Thank you for coming today."

She beckons us inside and mama and I wish her a good afternoon. As she takes our coats the smell of baking wafts through from the kitchen into the passageway. This would ordinarily entice me but today I have no appetite. I couldn't even manage a peck of food at breakfast.

In the kitchen Lilian and Sissy are waiting at the table. Strangely I'm taken aback even though I was expecting to see them. The sisters scramble to their feet when we enter the room and I notice even Lilian has made a special effort with her appearance. Lilian—the name has been locked in my thoughts for five years. Our likeness is remarkable, but I never think of her as my mother.

The atmosphere is thickened by unease as we exchange pleasantries and Elspeth extends her hand to the two well-worn chairs by the range.

Nothing has changed since I was last in the kitchen except perhaps new curtains, but I can't be sure. I loved this room, I think, my throat catching at the memory of a time when everything was different. I thought I had found new friends, friends who felt like family. The irony is jarring.

Elspeth is jabbering about the chilly weather and the chance of rain as she pours the tea and slices a Victoria sponge cake. We all gladly take tea but politely decline the cake in turn. We're all clearly feeling the same. Elspeth looks crestfallen as though the key to a successful afternoon has been snatched from her. Oh, if only cake was the key.

"Well, perhaps you might fancy a slice later," she says, still hopeful, then sits at the beautifully presented table with her daughters.

The divide between the two factions is apparent though unintentional and I wonder if Elspeth wishes she'd thought of it.

Yet again I know I must be the one to start the conversation where we left off. Elspeth turns her attention to me when she hears me clearing my throat.

"Thank you for the invitation, Elspeth," I say. "I'm glad to be here today though I know it's difficult for everyone."

I glance at mama who remains impassively staring at the floor, her pallor sickly.

Elspeth is tracing the flowers of the tablecloth with her fingertips.

"Sissy and Lilian would like to talk to you, wouldn't you girls?" she says without looking up.

The sisters nod in unison. The similarities between the two women have lessened over the years. Sissy is almost grey and more rounded whilst Lilian seems years younger than the short age gap between them. Lilian is the one to break the silence.

"I know I've caused a lot of upset and I'm sorrier about it than you can ever know. Me and Sissy want to tell you what happened all those years ago as we think you should know. It seems you would like to hear our story as you're here today."

She sounds so wooden, highlighted by her rigid jawline. I wonder if she's rehearsed what she wants to say, and the thought somehow touches me.

"Lilian's right," Sissy says, "There's so many things been left unsaid. I think it would be a relief to say them, not just for you, Annalise but for all of us."

Lilian shows a hint of a smile then glances at her sister. Sissy's opening was clearly rehearsed.

"Do you want to start, Sissy or shall I?" she asks.

"You start and then I'll join in," Sissy says politely.

They appear so civilised with one another as though the fracas between them never happened. I picture them as young girls living here and wonder about their relationship then. Did the lie ruin them or were they always sisters at war?

Lilian takes a swig of tea then a deep breath. I suddenly realise all her hopes hang on her next words and wager the burden is weighing heavily.

"Well then, I need to start somewhere. For Annalise's benefit: If you recall Mrs Whitworth, Stevie told your husband all those years ago about a young lass who was pregnant with nowhere to turn. Mr Whitworth then told Stevie you would both like to adopt the baby if the girl was agreeable."

Mama nods but still doesn't look at me or anyone else. The flush of her pale cheeks contrasts like bloodstains on snow.

"Then your husband rented the cottage for me, and I left my job telling mam I'd got myself a position as a lady-in-waiting at your house. I told her that Stevie had recommended me to Mr Whitworth, and I couldn't wait to start. This was the first lie I told," she glances at her mother, "Mam knows the whole sorry story now though, so nothing will come as a shock."

Elspeth pats her daughter's hand gently. The family have done so much healing in the intervening years by the look of things, far more than my family has. Perhaps this is the silver lining of the cloud.

"I lived at the cottage until the baby was due," Lilian goes on, "and then I said I wanted my sister to help me with the birth. It was all agreed."

Lilian pauses for so long, mama is forced to say in a broken voice, "Yes, I remember."

Looking over at her mother Lilian seems to be seeking some kind of encouragement or reassurance to resume the story. Elspeth's eyes are circles as she nods her head.

"This bit is hard to tell you because I regret it so much," Lilian says, "as does Sissy," she adds quickly.

231

Clara shoots Sissy a look and asks: "What has Sissy got to do with anything?"

Lilian's face flushes as pink as mamas as I watch mama now shuffle around in her seat with agitation.

"You see," Lilian says, "you see, Mrs Whitworth … it wasn't me who was pregnant."

Mama shakes her head, her expression changing from incredulity to annoyance. I know my mother; I know she's fast losing tolerance of all the playing around with the facts.

"Then if it wasn't you …" mama says, her voice trailing to nothing.

I watch her mouth grow wide into a great chasm, her eyes flashing between all of us.

"You!" mama almost shouts, "are you telling me now that you are Annalise's mother?"

Sissy looks terrified by mama's reaction. They stare at each other until Sissy finally yields to look at the stone flags of the floor.

One single nod of Sissy's head is enough to break mama and she starts to weep but not softly. A shuddering noise escapes her and I'd like to go to her but I'm unable to move.

"You are my mother," I whisper.

It's a statement not a question.

Raising her chin Sissy exhales a long breath and looks into my eyes for the very first time. I know she is my mother, I can feel it in a way I never could with Lilian. It all seems so terribly obvious now.

"Yes, it's true, I'm your mother. I can't begin to explain how upset I've been to live a lie your whole life," she turns to Clara who's wiping her eyes, "but also, I'm sorry to do this to you, Mrs Whitworth. I only hope you can both at least believe me when I say this even if you can never forgive me."

A tear rolls down Sissy's face and drops onto the bodice of her dress. I feel a pain in my chest so pointedly it takes my breath away. I fight the urge to take the short walk to comfort her but only because I don't want to upset mama.

The room falls silent as we sit with our individual thoughts, trying to line them up properly.

"Are you alright, mama?" I ask eventually.

She looks my way briefly.

"Not really but I'd like to get to the end of the story if we may," she says.

Elspeth fills her teacup, and I see them exchange glances which are compassionate if not affectionate. Elspeth was not part of her daughters' plan.

"It was my idea," Sissy says, "I asked Lilian to lie and say the baby—you, Annalise—were hers. She had Stevie to turn to and we didn't know how he would help but we knew he would. We thought at first that he might help us find a stranger to adopt the baby, this seemed the logical solution. Never in our wildest dreams did we think you and Mr Whitworth would be the ones who wanted to adopt. Of course, we had no way of knowing you wanted a baby so badly, Mrs Whitworth, but it seemed like fate had dealt us the perfect solution. Now I can only hope you'll let me try and explain why I was so desperate."

I nod, as does mama in my peripheral vision. I think we're both as keen as each other to learn how a woman could give up their baby when they were married. It doesn't make sense, seeming so selfish and needless.

"Few people know but my husband Samuel who died three years ago was a cruel man. I often think I've failed even to convince mam and Lily because it's difficult to put into words how he made me feel. He was subtle about it, so I didn't notice at first but over time he made my self-worth slip away until I didn't recognise myself. All I wanted to do was please him and my two boys— your brothers—but it was impossible to please a man like him. He was my husband, but I never thought of him as your father. I will always be glad you never met him, and my only comfort is that he got his comeuppance in the end.

It was easier to hide the pregnancy as, to be candid, as he barely touched me by then. Barely being the important word here. We'd been sleeping in separate beds for years but even so when I found out I was going to have a baby I was worried he might visit me one night after the pub. I decided to tell him I had 'women's trouble' and that did the trick in keeping him at arm's length. In any case I doubt it was much of a loss for him. I never knew or cared if he had other women on the side, but I wouldn't have put it past him.

The only thing I knew for certain was a baby would not help the terrible life I was living. I was going to leave Samuel so our Lily and me could live together. We could just about afford it between us, but we couldn't afford another mouth to feed. Those were desperate times; I was a different person."

Sissy pauses and her bottom lip trembles. Elspeth touches her arm, and they exchange glances, her mother nodding encouragement.

"I thought I would be able to just let you go and forget you. I'm ashamed to say now that for a while I did, only relieved to have found you a good home. But over the years you crept into my thoughts quite gently at some point during the day. I'd seen you from time to time of course so I knew what you looked like but it wasn't enough. My thoughts grew about the kind of girl you had grown into then the kind of woman you'd become. Your birthdays and Christmases were difficult days.

She hangs her head, her body crumpling like its lost its stuffing.

"For my part, when I started to live in the cottage, I found I liked it more than I could ever have imagined," Lilian interjects, "I liked my independence, my freedom, and I quickly discovered so much about myself. I knew I couldn't leave that life behind," she looks at her sister then at the floor, "so I went back on my offer. I left Sissy and the boys high and dry."

She takes a swig of cold tea, slapping her cup down on her saucer with enough force to make me jump.

"It's been six of one, half a dozen of the other," Sissy says, "You helped me out when I needed you, Lily, but I should never have asked you, never mind had the… Annalise adopted. I know now I could have moved in here or found a job and a small place. The boys would have helped me out eventually as they went out to work. But I didn't want to lose face and I couldn't see past the bitterness. So, over the years the bitterness left a mark so deep it became a scar I could never be rid of, I was stuck with it. I couldn't see anything other than resentment for my sister and the life she loved. I felt like Lily had stolen my life and my identity. I didn't stop to think for a minute that I'd asked her to do it in the first place, that she'd lied to help me. I only knew that she was happy and content, or she would have been if we'd left her alone, and I was stuck in my miserable marriage without my daughter. It all seemed for nothing, and Lily was the winner. That's when after more than two decades of torture it all came to a head. I lost my mind for a while that night and I shall never forgive myself for my behaviour."

She buries her head in her hands and I'm reminded briefly of that night and all the others after I went to bed thinking she was my aunt and not my mother.

Now my mother's sobs play with my heartstrings, and I want it to stop. I almost go to her side but then watch with relief as mama gets up and slides her arms around Sissy's shoulders, crouching at her feet to look up at her face contorted from weeping.

"Listen carefully to me, Sissy, we've all made mistakes in this situation and one way or another we've all let Annalise down. But as you pointed out, you were desperate and the way I see it your sham of a life wasn't your own doing. Your husband has a lot to answer for and no doubt is doing so now, so is it any wonder you lost your mind when the plan you made with Lilian went array? As for me, I must tell you I've had the pleasure of being Annalise's mother and for this alone I shall be forever indebted to you."

I resist the urge to wrap my arms around the two of them as one—my mama and my mother united in their pain. I know I must give them a moment of their own. As a mother myself now, I know this.

"I agree with mama," I say eventually as four faces turn to look at me, "we must try and move on from all this after today. We must try because it's time. I've had a happy life with loving parents, so things turned out well in the end. I also found what I considered to be dear friends," I look at each woman in turn, "Just because they turned out to be my mother, my grandmother, and my aunt doesn't mean they can't still be dear friends even if it takes a little while."

Sissy's bombshell has been a revelation and far from a tidy conclusion. I picture her as a young woman with two young sons, shackled with a tyrant of a husband.

"Who knows what I would have done in your shoes, Sissy. I've been blessed with a loving husband so I could never know," I say.

We share our first genuine smile and it warms me.

Standing up Sissy pulls mama gently to her full height but towers over her. Holding onto her hands she says, "I know I got lucky, I left my daughter in good hands. I saw that the first time I met you, though it would have choked me to admit it then."

A tiny ripple of laughter joins us as a complete circle for the very first time. The atmosphere of the room has changed, it cements my sense that we're all ready to move on to the next stage of our lives.

"I think we all needed to get to this place in our hearts and minds," mama says locking eyes with Elspeth, "If one of us wasn't ready then none of us could have been. We are four women bound by our love for Annalise. So many lies have been told, so much time lost to worry and guilt, we have all been damaged by it."

Sissy and Lilian listen to mama's speech from their seats at the table, hanging on to her every word.

Mama turns her attention to them, saying, "It's a pleasure to see you both reconciled, it seems you have reached an understanding at least which is no mean feat. You should be proud the damage didn't break your relationship once and for all."

The sisters smile coyly at one another, then Sissy shakes her head.

"Now, don't get too carried away," she says, "we still have our moments, we're sisters when all said and done. But I'd say we've found a way to live and let live."

"Well, it was that or bury the hatchet… in the back of your head," Lilian says with a small chuckle.

The room is filled with the joyful laughter of a band of women who have somehow managed to free themselves of the shackles they put on themselves.

Mama looks my way as we laugh. We both have tears in our eyes, and I'd like to leave to be alone with her so we can discuss the day's events. She's had so much insecurity from the first day she held me in her arms as a baby until this very day. She will have lived with the constant fear of me being taken from her when I am the centre of her world, like Florence is the centre of mine. Even as we laugh now, I feel certain the worry of being replaced or diminished in my affections is still loitering in the back of her mind.

Soon we will leave here together but I know we shall return. Soon I can take my dear mama into my arms and hold her tightly. Then I can hold her at arm's length and look deeply into her eyes so she can never doubt the truth. I will tell her she is my role model as a mother, and I hope to be half the mother to Florence as she has been to me.

Then I will be content.

Come what may, one thousand Sissy's could never replace my one beloved mama.

Chapter 31

1902 - Annalise

I lean out of the carriage window calling, "Burton, please will you take a detour to Cavendish Road?"

My words seem to fly into the wind, but Burton catches them calling over his shoulder, "Certainly, madam."

Settling back in the carriage seat I relive my conversation with mama and papa before I left Hardcastle. For the first time possibly in my life mama looked at ease, the contours of her face softened, her eyes aglow so she looked…happy. Yes, I would say happy.

Secrets and lies have been part of my parents' lives since I was born. I notice papa is quieter nowadays, but people change as they go through life. I've changed and so has Hugo. We're not the same people but luckily, we're still as one. Perhaps luck is a big part to play in the longevity of love, it's quite easy to love someone for a while.

"I hope in time we can all forget this," papa said.

Mama looked between the two of us.

"I'm not sure if we can or should forget. We must learn from situations good and bad in our lives and sit with them. Our pasts mould us. Trying to forget them entirely is a burden we can take from our own shoulders. Acceptance is key I think."

How sage she is; how I love her.

"Indeed," I said, as papa nodded his agreement, his face softened by his own love for this woman we're both lucky to have in our lives.

"I must tell you what I told mama," I said to papa, "I've been in hiding sometimes these past years. I've thrown myself into wifehood, motherhood and running the house because I haven't wanted to face my emotions. They've been too raw to delve into and I'm sorry you've missed out on Florence more than you should have."

Papa looked choked and lost for words.

"I'm sure I've had a far better life than I would have done being born into a loveless marriage. You and mama have given me a wonderful life and I could not have been loved more. I have nothing but gratitude for both of you."

Crossing the hearth rug, I sat by my father's side and took both his hands in mine.

"Thank you, papa," is all I said but his eyes demonstrated he knew the magnitude of the sentiment behind my words.

I spot the sign for Cavendish Street and smile. Today is a day for moving forward but I must finish my old life properly.

After Burton helps me from the carriage, I head to knock on the door of number fifty. The door is still the same colour but a little tattier than I remember. I glance up and down the road, the wind blowing detritus in all directions and keeping people snug in their homes. It takes a moment or two before I hear shuffling steps in the hallway and the key turning.

Rheumy blue eyes peer through the gap. I wait and watch the expression in them change slowly from bewilderment at who could possibly be visiting this afternoon to one of pure delight.

"Annalise!" Mr Greenacre exclaims, throwing the door wide.

"I hope you don't mind me dropping in on you unexpectedly, Mr Greenacre."

The years drop away from him as he grins my way.

"I knew you would come one day soon, so you are the most expected of unexpected visitors. Come inside out of this dreadful wind, my dear."

The scent of the house hits me as I step into the hallway. It's evocative, powerful, so much so I must breathe deeply a few times to compose myself. I feel I'm drowning in the memories, and they are being replayed like flashlights in my mind. Following Mr Greenacre into the music room is almost my undoing, it's as though I left the room only yesterday.

"I thought we might sit in here," he says, "This is the one room Mrs Greenacre left untouched at my request. I clean it once a week religiously mind, even now."

He says it proudly and I smile affectionately at him as we sit in our usual seats.

"I'm sorry I haven't visited since Mrs Greenacre's funeral," I tell him, "I've … I've not been quite myself these last few years, but this is a poor excuse I know."

"Would a cup of tea make everything better?" he asks.

I really don't want to waste time him making and us drinking tea, I think. I only want to talk to him.

"No, that's quite alright thank you. I'm quite awash today," I say.

He picks up his empty pipe and puffs away. His wife may have gone but he's still respecting her wishes I see. My lips twitch and his eyes twinkle with our shared old joke.

"Why is today the day you chose to come and see me?" he asks.

I'm not startled by the lack of preamble to the conversation. This is how he is and how I like him to be.

I take off my hat and coat and place them on the back of the chair as he watches me, pipe in mouth.

"Today is the day I free myself from my old self."

He doesn't speak or ask what I mean. It sounds silly, like a riddle, and I don't want to speak in riddles. This was never us. In this room we could be frank and open without fear of reproach or judgement.

Sighing I look my mentor straight and true in the eye.

"Some years ago, before Florence was born, I discovered I was adopted. I've been coming to terms with the deception since that day. Today my birth grandmother asked mama and I to visit, and we did. I think it will turn out to be one of the best decisions I ever made."

He doesn't show shock or any emotion whatsoever, even compassion.

"I see. This explains our very first open discussion when you were sixteen years old about feeling an outsider. How perceptive you turned out to be."

I glance at the piano and remember how mediocre I was at playing.

"And you," I say, "now Mrs Greenacre is no longer with us have you been tempted to reach out to your family," I ask.

"Every day," he says without hesitation.

"Will you?"

"Let us discuss your situation first if we may. Have you turned your back on professional singing altogether?"

I stare into the fire, recalling the day the ground shifted only a short while ago.

"Well, it's true, I thought I had until around six weeks ago. Florence has started tutoring sessions for five hours a day and Hugo was writing in his study. I had a feeling of boredom which I hadn't had in a long time. I went to the music room, which is nowhere near as wonderful as this room by the way, and I began to sing. Not quietly to myself which I do often, I went through the scales, then I sang the first aria I ever sang at the *Royal Opera House*. Do you remember?"

He nods but doesn't say anything sentimental such as "How could I forget?" or "Such a wonderful moment." This is why I enjoy our measured conversations as I do.

"Well, in that moment I knew I wasn't finished with singing. I can't go back to the old way of life, but I can reach for somewhere in between. Mr Bamford told Howie he could fill the opera house tomorrow, but I'd rather sing in more intimate settings. I grew to enjoy them more and I realise I'm in the fortunate position where I can do as few or as many as I like."

"So, you'd like a balance?" he asked.

"Exactly. One day I'm sure I will be only too glad to walk away from opera singing but I think I have a few more years in me yet."

He laughs, his eyes folding at the edges, his mouth wide and for once I'm taken aback.

"Yes, my dear, I think you have a few more years yet," he says.

I join his laughter and feel a release so intensely it can easily turn to tears of hysteria if I'm not careful.

Shovelling more coal on the fire, Mr Greenacre sits back down, and I know now is the time.

"I have a performance at Christmas and some special people are attending. It would be a great honour if you would accompany me for the whole evening or just one piece if you prefer?"

His eyes narrow as he looks at me. I know what he's thinking because I know him so well.

"I would be delighted," he says.

I'm sure his initial reaction will have been to decline my offer, but this would only be from fear of failure. I know he's good enough and after pushing past his fears in only seconds, he now knows it too. He has guided me many times in this way.

"Will you reach out to your family?" I ask again.

He reaches for his empty pipe once more.

"Tomorrow I will know the answer," he says.

"But tomorrow can never come," I tell him.

"I have given myself a deadline of tomorrow today. Tomorrow I will know the answer," he repeats.

Glancing out of the window I remember the real world is out there and I must return to it. The day has been long.

"I must go," I say, "If you're agreeable I could return tomorrow with Florence to see if she has a better aptitude for piano than her mother."

"You may return, of course, but my dear Annalise I shall not be rushed."

"I've missed you is all, nothing more and I'd like to make up for lost time. I shall never ask you about reconciling with your family again," I say as he helps me put on my coat.

I follow him to the front door but before he opens it, he turns to me.

"I take it the special guests you are referring to are your new family," he says, "I shall look forward to meeting them."

"Yes, it would give me great deal of pleasure to have them there," I pause to think of someone, "There is one person, a special man who has played a significant part in my story who I may need to persuade to attend, but I hope he will agree. I have a great deal to thank him for and I shall in my own way."

He holds my gaze a moment and I wonder what he wants to say.

"You know, I read in The Times you have great riches now yet you have never offered me any money whatsoever."

I smile but don't look away.

"That is because you would be greatly insulted and would think our relationship sullied."

He reaches to place his warm palm gently on my forearm, his expression grave.

"And that, my dear is part of the light within you I saw beaming my way the first day you walked into my house when you were barely fourteen years old. "Emmanuele, you old fool," I said to myself, "I don't know how you can possibly know, but this young girl is going to change the world one day … and not for the worse.""

Chapter 32

1902 - Stevie

Elspeth can't help smiling to herself when she hears Stevie whistling as he comes in the gate.

He only stops whistling when he sees her standing at the range holding his tea on a plate with a tea towel as an oven glove. She packed him off to the pub whilst they had their little gathering, and he looks as though he's had a very pleasant afternoon she thinks.

"Ah, here she is, the little woman," he says a grin splitting his face from ear to ear.

Pursing her lips Elspeth raises her eyebrows.

"Be careful, mister or you might find this dinner on your head making comments like that."

He draws her into his arms for a lingering kiss and she curls her fingers into his thick copper hair. Oh, this man is all man and he's all mine she thinks. She's in no rush to pull away.

"You can go to the pub more often if this is the effect it has on you," she whispers into his neck.

Stevie sits down at the table to have his tea, his eyes lighting up at the pie and mash smothered in Elspeth's special gravy.

"So, how did it go?" he asks.

She joins him in the seat opposite, too excited to eat this night.

"It couldn't have gone better to be honest," she tells him, "You could have knocked me down with a feather duster when Mr Burton appeared with the note to accept my invitation; I've had a few sleepless nights wondering if Annalise would even respond never mind accept."

What you never have you never miss Elspeth thinks but now she's found her granddaughter it would have been like losing one of her daughters. She closes her eyes briefly at the terrible thought.

Oblivious, Stevie scoops his peas with his upturned fork and shovels them into his mouth. Elspeth looks on fondly. He loves his food and Elspeth loves spoiling him and not just with food. He's never had a home before here, he told her once and that's another terrible thought.

"Are they coming again?" he asks, taking a swig of tea from his pint pot mug.

"Next Saturday so you might want to go to the pub for a bit of peace. She's meeting Jack and Harry. I'm sure it won't put you out too much."

Stevie smiles at his wife, pleased to see that glow she lost for so long is back. One meeting with the right outcome has lit up her face again.

"You know, Annalise has decided to do the odd performance in London again. She says she's missed it, but it will only be a few times a year. She's asked us all to go down and see a performance near Christmas. You can come if you like, she's putting us up in some posh hotel."

Stevie wipes his mouth on his napkin Elspeth insists on him using and sits back in his chair.

"What and steal your thunder. No, you go and be with your girls, you'll love it."

Her girls; such a heart-warming turn of phrase.

"I think it might be important to her that you come too, Stevie."

They stare across the table at each other and he reads her mind but doesn't say anything. I suppose I'll go in that case, he thinks, though I can't abide a fuss.

Elspeth's mind goes to Sissy. She's happy enough now Samuel's gone but she was walking about with a piece missing for so long, Elspeth had to do something about it.

Now she has her granddaughter and great granddaughter in the fold and all's right in her world again.

She heaps custard over the bread-and-butter pudding she made this morning. His face is like sunshine when she puts the bowl in front on him.

"By, you know the way to man's heart, love," he says, making her laugh.

Elspeth listens to the rise and fall of the sound of children playing in the street as she relives the events of today. She knows it will be long time before she stops reliving this day.

"Does Annalise know about her mother ... about Clara?" Stevie asks between mouthfuls of pudding.

Shaking her head Elspeth shifts in her seat, her face flushing pink.

"No, but then there might not be anything to know. She could be here for years yet, so I understand why she doesn't want Annalise to live with the thought hanging over her head. She looked pale mind."

"Does Garrison know?" Stevie asks.

"Nobody knows except me and you, not even our Sissy and Lilian. Clara wanted Annalise to have us by her side if anything happened to her, that's the long and the short of it though she hasn't said it. Can you imagine not knowing from one minute to the next if your heart will pack in? No wonder she reached out to me after so long. I'd almost given up hope, it just shows, we should never lose faith."

"Ay, it's true. Five years is a long time to wait," Stevie says placing his bowl in the sink.

Settling himself in his chair by the fire he lights his pipe. She remembers how she worried about the age gap once upon a time but now she knows he's an old head on young shoulders.

"Who would have thought I'd live long enough to be a great grandmother? How do you feel about that?" she asks him.

She sounds like she's joking but can't help her stomach dropping. They had the conversation about him missing out on children years ago, but he's always been adamant it's not something he dwells on. Perhaps Florence might fill the void if they see more of her, though the void may well be in her imagination.

"I think you're the classiest, most good-looking great grandma I've ever set eyes on. I'll show you how I feel about it later."

Chuckling, her mind settles down as she joins him in her chair, watching him enjoy his pipe. She thinks of him as a simple soul in the best sense.

"I've been saving a bit of news myself until after your gathering," he says.

"I hope it's good news because I'd hate my bubble to be popped today, Stevie."

His expression gives nothing away, so she holds her breath.

"You just so happen to be looking at the new gaffer of *Garrison Whitworth and Sons Ltd.*"

Elspeth's jaw hangs: well, he kept that one quiet she thinks. It's no more than he deserves because he's dedicated his life to that man and that place since he was fourteen years old. Garrison knew a good thing when he saw it and he still knows it now.

"Oh love, I'm made up for you, I really am. Nobody works harder—credit to you."

Putting his pipe on the side table he lifts her from her seat and wraps his arms around her.

"I'm made up for both of us. Life can change now in any way you like; we could even move house. Garrison says he wants to spend more time with his family, so he won't be in the office as much and needs a manager, someone he can trust to run things day to day. I forget how old he is sometimes because he never seems to age, not really. If I'm honest I can't believe what he's paying me, I feel as though we'll never be able to spend it."

"Oh, don't you worry, we'll have a good go," Elspeth laughs, "But why would I want l move from this house when everything I want is here."

She reaches on tiptoes to kiss him, and he responds in a way which leaves her in no doubt about how much he loves her, his body sinking into hers.

Eventually she pulls away to look at him, remembering something from earlier in the day.

"Would you believe Hugo has asked if he can write our story, under different names of course? He thinks it would be very popular, and I'm inclined to agree but he said he would only write it with our permission. I don't think Annalise was joking when she told us. Clara made what everyone else thought was a joke when she said he could publish it after she was gone. I wasn't laughing."

"No, that's not funny," he says, "Maybe she has a deep dark secret she would hate to be discovered; the quiet ones are always worst."

They look at each other in such a way he wishes he could swallow the words back down. They both know this to be true.

The one thing to cloud the horizon is the ever-present nag at the back of their minds they might one day get a knock at the door. It's been three years but it still nags at them.

They knew they had no choice in the end but to help Sissy. Samuel would have lived forever even with his bad chest, so they had to step in; she was drinking herself to death and it was the lesser of two evils.

They were extremely careful about how they went about it of course, just topping his medicine with water little by little, so he steadily declined. Nobody was any the wiser and if they think about it logically nobody ever could be. But if the knock should come, Stevie will take full responsibility. He will do what it takes to protect his family as he always has even before he married Elspeth. In their own way they all love him dearly for it. Sissy has no idea, and how he hopes she never will.

"So, what would the title of Hugo's book be, I wonder," Stevie says, pulling his wife's hair loose, trying to rid them both of the thoughts tarnishing their mood, "*The Five Formidable Women.*"

He chuckles softly into the top of her head.

"Don't forget Florence," she says, "it will have to be something like *The Six Sensational Women.*"

"And who could argue with that?" he says tracing his finger down the side of her cheek. He knows it's flushed just from the nearness of him and that's a wonderful thought, one that makes him feel wanted, cherished even.

When she eventually turns from him, he catches a glimpse of the factory window from which he used to watch this little kitchen-sink drama from afar. He's glad Elspeth knows all about it now.

Does he still think of the days of Garrison Whitworth? Undoubtedly, but this has lessened over the years, and he knows the love he has with his wife is real; so real.

Now he will forever thank his lucky stars he has somehow, someway been fortunate enough to be cast as the leading man in Elspeth's life.

And he has no doubt in his mind it was the part he was born to play to the end of his days.

Printed in Great Britain
by Amazon